MW00932264

Published by Imagination Unlimited LLC

Love Cuffs
ISBN 9781535467131
ALL RIGHTS RESERVED.
Love Cuffs Original Copyright © 2008 Ashlyn Chase
& Dalton Diaz
Rewritten and republished 2016
Original Version Edited by Helen Woodall.
Cover art by Syneca Featherstone
Formatted by Enterprise Book Services, LLC

Dedication

Dedicated to our late mothers. We make fun of Faith's mother in this book, but that in no way resembles the relationships we had with our wonderful mothers...two of the best people to have ever walked the earth.
—Ashlyn

Dedicated to Cindy for more than I can say. Not many people would cross state lines, paintbrush in hand, to help someone they barely know. You are a true friend.

To J: You promised me the world. You've given me the universe.
—Dalton

Ashlyn Chase & Dalton Diaz

Acknowledgements

A huge shout out and thank you goes to Dalton Diaz. I could not have written this book without her!

Once again, I must acknowledge my funny lawyer, Richard Leonard J.D. for relating the true story that inspired this one. Yes, believe it or not, a small part of this insane tale is rooted in truth.

I must also acknowledge fellow author Cynnara Tregarth for contributing her expert opinions and research into the psychology of BDSM.
—Ashlyn

I have to acknowledge fellow author and friend, Samantha Cayto. Definitely interesting research. (Raising bag of peanut M&M's in honor.) This Club's for you.
—Dalton

Author Note

This story is in no way a serious view of the BDSM life style and culture. Sit back, relax and enjoy it with a smile.

Warning: This book contains graphic language, sex scenes, and mature content. Again...enjoy!

Prologue

It all began six months ago while I was camping in the Smoky Mountains with Morty the accountant. I know he wasn't exactly the most exciting person but I'd had a long dry spell and my standards had sort of slipped.

As I crawled out of my sleeping bag, trying not to disturb him, he woke up anyway and asked, "Are you okay?"

"I'm fine," I said. "I just have to go...um..."

"Water a bush?" he asked.

"Yeah, thanks for putting it delicately." Now being a cop, I was used to overhearing crass comments but coming from a date I didn't feel particularly fond of—*ick*. Now that I didn't have to worry about disturbing him, I scrambled out of my sleeping bag built for one, *thank goodness,* threw on my jeans and sneakers then pulled a sweatshirt over my head. As I unzipped the tent flap, I said, "Be back in a flash."

I stepped into the crisp night air and wished I didn't have to come back at all. The sky, studded with stars held me captive and the smoky smell of the previous night's campfire lingered in the air. Oh well…might as well take care of business and enjoy the evening on my way back. I trotted toward the woods, pine needles cushioning my feet and the smell reminding me of winter holiday candles. Some experiences are just too beautiful to be shared with an accountant named Morty.

I went to the little girl's room—more like little girl's stump—did what I had to do and slowly strolled back toward the tent. A twig snapped behind me and I froze. Turning slowly, I squinted into the darkness. Two golden glowing eyes at about the level of my kneecaps stared back at me. *Holy crap…*

"Morty," I called. There was no answer. "Mooorty! We have company," I sang.

A low growl reverberated from the direction of the eyes that had been trained on me. They were no longer visible. I glanced around nervously, trying to locate the mysterious eyes. When I spotted them, I noticed they were moving around me. A shape came into view as the figure crept forward.

"Morty?" I raised my voice. "I think you'd better put on your sneakers and get ready to run."

"Why?" he called back. "What's going on?"

I was hoping for a dog. No such luck. This doggie was overly large, black as the night, shaggy and drooling. *Crap.* Slowly, very slowly, I backed up toward the tent although I was still well into the woods. I heard the distant zip of the tent flap. A flashlight beam darted around the woods finally focusing on my backside and more importantly, the wolf coming toward me.

"Holy shit," Morty yelped. Suddenly the beam of

light disappeared and I heard the pitter patter of running feet in the opposite direction. I heard his voice from far away yelling, "I'll go get help."

Terrific, thanks a bunch. I'll just stay here and see what old Wolfie has in mind for me. "Nice boy. Nice wolf." I automatically reached for my invisible weapon and cursed the empty spot at my side where it should have been. Coolly, I scanned the ground for something I could use to defend myself.

A good-sized flat rock lay near my foot so I slowly crouched down and reached for it. That's when he launched himself at me.

I managed to grab the rock and wedge it into his teeth so he couldn't close his jaws. Did he have to slobber so much? He drooled all over my hands! Those damn teeth looked sharp and I didn't plan to stick around to find out how much they'd hurt as they sank into my thigh.

I whirled around, pushed my heels into the dirt and took off. I only had seconds to escape. Ahead of me, I spotted a tree with a low branch I could reach so I beat feet toward the tree, pulling my tomboy self off the ground just in time. As he leapt for the branch, I scurried up to the next one.

Scrambling up the tree as far as I could, I wedged myself into a good spot and glanced back down. He made a couple of futile jumps, then seemed to give up. Kind of. He sat on his haunches, staring up at me. What was even more infuriating was how he cocked his head, as if wondering why I didn't climb back down and just slide into his mouth. "Oh, you'd like that wouldn't you, Wolfie?"

I awaited my rescue…and waited and waited. *Where the frig is everybody?* I expected the park rangers, animal control, cops and an ambulance. Hell, I'd even take the ski patrol at this point. Anyone with a stun gun or tranquilizer dart would be nice. But nooo...we were stuck in a stalemate. At last, Wolfie began to howl. He bayed incessantly as if he too had waited a little too long for back-up.

By now I was going slightly insane, so I straddled a branch and kicked my feet like a four year old, fingers in my ears, singing la la la la... Finally, dawn began to creep over the Smoky Mountains. Wolfie paced, looking nervous. He stopped howling and glanced around. Then, he took off into the woods—at last!

I waited another good ten minutes in the tree, still hoping for some kind of professional rescuer when I decided I was on my own. I had been deserted. I climbed back down, returned to the tent, pulled out the things that belonged to me and rolled them up in my sleeping bag. Finally I strapped on my backpack, opened a bag of trail mix and hiked down the mountain, popping raisins into my mouth as if nothing had happened.

Chapter One

In any relationship, there's one's truth, the other's truth and the real truth

A lot can change in six months and that applied to me. For one thing, I had developed this bizarre ability to hear things right through walls or from several blocks away. Another thing that had happened was my engagement. Not to Morty. Don't worry I'm not that crazy. But now, sitting in the function hall's side dressing room with my maid of honor, Kat, I glanced at myself in the mirror for about the twentieth time. Who was that? She looked kind of like me. She had my long blonde hair but a curling iron and lots of hairspray had plastered it into a much prettier hairstyle than my usual braids or bun. Hair and tulle tickled my arms. In a strapless, white lace gown with some makeup and blush I looked pretty damn good.

Kat, hands on her hips, clucked her tongue. "Faith. I can't believe you're going through with this. Are you sure you're not just settling? Somehow I can't see you married."

"What's that supposed to mean?"

"No offense or anything. You just don't seem to need a man. I thought you didn't believe in marriage."

I shrugged. Truth be told, I really didn't know what I was doing. In retrospect, this whole thing seemed like a last-ditch effort. I wasn't getting any younger at thirty-eight and counting. Better to get married before nobody wanted me. Besides, there was a dearth of unattached Jewish men my age or slightly older and usually a good reason they were still available. Forget marrying a non-Jew. My parents would have a gefilte-fit!

Kat was speaking again. I had to pull myself back to reality and focus on what she was saying.

"It's not too late you know. I don't care that I spent two hundred dollars for this midnight blue confection of satin ruffles that I'll never wear again." She looked down at her gown, which I had to admit was not her at all. No more than this white wedding cake I was wearing was me. My mother had picked everything out. I just wanted a simple ceremony by a Justice of the Peace but she freaked. She took over and arranged absolutely everything right down to my hairstyle.

As if on cue, my controlling mom bustled in. "Oh, darling, you look so beautiful. Did I not tell you this is the perfect dress? Now make sure to stand up straight when you walk down the aisle so no one thinks your boobs are already sagging."

I rolled my eyes. "Yes, Mother."

"And you, Katerina, shouldn't fill her with false hopes of finding Mr. Right. She should count her lucky stars that Roger isn't that picky. She's thirty-eight and I'd like to have a grandchild or two while I still have my health."

"Not picky? Mother!"

"I'm just saying…" She glanced at her watch and sang out, "Oh, it's almost time…" With her hands fluttering in the air, she hurried back from whence she came.

Good. The woman could drive me from zero to crazy in sixty seconds.

I stared into the mirror again. "We look good, right, Kat?"

Kat rolled her eyes. "This is not about looking good, Faith. This is about committing the rest of your life to someone you barely know. You bumped into an old boyfriend you knew twenty years ago and suddenly you're engaged? Something must have happened right before he asked you. Did you hit your head or something?"

"Nope."

"Have you thought about why you broke up? Remember what happened to piss you off all those years ago."

"I'm over that."

"Should you be? He cheated on you."

"We were eighteen."

"And what if he doesn't like kids and you want some? God knows your mother certainly does. Have you talked about that?"

"Um. Not exactly," I said, sheepishly.

Kat looked like she wanted to pull her hair out. Curls and all. "Just think about it, all right? It's not too late."

"Kat, you're my best friend. The most honest one I've ever had and you're making too much sense. Please stop it. I don't want to get mad at you on my wedding day."

Regardless of how close we were, I had never told her about the new heightened auditory sense I had added ever since the Wolfie incident. I don't know why but I suspected it might have had something to do with that wolf's saliva and stuffing my fingers in my ears. How nutty would that sound? But, ever since then, I've had to wear earplugs hidden by my hair to keep from hearing every lewd comment whispered behind my back—even after closing the door!

It was especially inconvenient at work where my coworkers were supposed to respect me. I really didn't need to know about how my ass looked from the back or how nicely it wiggled as I left the room. And just to make things worse, I had to put my hair in some kind of style that wouldn't get in my way and in order to hide the earplugs I had to wear pigtails. I'm sure that didn't help garner respect. Fortunately the badge was enough for the public but remarks about being backed up by Pippi Longstocking were just too much. So the earplugs were welcome when I was working or any time I didn't want to hear what people were saying about me in the next room. Even friends and family just suck sometimes.

That wasn't the case today. I looked damn good and I wanted to hear everybody's compliments. I also wanted to hear any catty remarks to know who my real friends were. So I removed my earplugs and stuffed them into my bra, which would go to Bermuda with me on my honeymoon. I mean, with us. I needed to get used to thinking in terms of being half of a couple. Not just me alone.

With a temple full of friends, family and coworkers I expected loads of oohs and ahhs. Even through the walls I could hear people murmuring to each other. "Oh I love that color lavender on you," my aunt was saying to someone. That could have meant, I love that color on you or I don't know what else to say and have forgotten your name.

I could hear my father greeting everyone as they came in the door as if he were a politician running for reelection. My socially conscious father, always with the smile and handshake for everyone else but harsh judgment and high expectations for me. I had to remind him that he had said I could be anything I wanted when I decided to go to the police academy.

Kat had even suggested that I was marrying Mr. Wrong as a way of both pleasing my mother now and pissing off my father later, after the divorce. That may be hard to comprehend but, believe it or not, I got it.

"What did you just stick in your bra?"

Damn. Kat never misses a thing. What the heck, I'd tell her everything. So I related the whole story about wolfie and my new auditory talent.

Her eyes rounded. "It was a werewolf."

She was kidding. She had to be kidding… She hadn't burst into laughter yet, and she was still wearing that 'just had a brow lift' expression. Oh, shit. She wasn't kidding.

"Kat—you know damn well there's no such thing as werewolves."

"How do you know?"

I huffed. "I just know."

"Spoken like a cop—everything is black and white."

"How about evidence? Every theory needs evidence before it can be proven true. Right?"

She rolled her eyes. "You are the evidence,

sweetheart."

Holy crap. If I thought it would do any good, I'd put my earplugs back in. Unfortunately, I couldn't unhear that.

"Be quiet and let me daydream about Bermuda."

My proud papa opened the door and I heard the *Wedding March* begin. I stood as if in a daze and walked toward the door, feeling as if I was walking to my execution. I blamed Kat for that.

As I entered the foyer, I heard a scream that halted me in my tracks. It came from outside somewhere.

"What's the matter honey?" My father frowned.

Kat came up beside me, resting her hand on my shoulder as another scream followed. I had two roles to play and I could only choose one. Blushing bride or the only cop who could hear this poor girl in trouble. I handed Kat my bouquet, hiked up my dress and charged down the temple steps.

"You go girl," Kat yelled after me. "Run, fly, be free!"

* * * * *

There was no time to call out an explanation over my shoulder since the screams sounded like they were coming from more than one person now and were increasing in intensity. I bolted toward the desperate sounds, which led me to the warehouse right across the street from the police station.

The ruckus seemed to be coming from the back of the adjacent alley. Not caring how dirt would cling to the hem of my dress after this sprint, I continued down the alley until I spotted a door at the top of some cement stairs. I grabbed the handle on a metal door and tugged. When it didn't open, I began pounding on it.

"Wow, somebody can't wait to get their freak on," I heard through the door. "Open it and see who it is." The voice sounded female but a man opened the door. At least I think it was a man. He stood about six feet tall, probably weighed two hundred fifty pounds and was wearing a leather bra and matching panties. The bulge indicated this was an anatomically correct male even though he filled out the bra with his man boobs.

"Kinky twist wearing a wedding dress," he said. "I like it."

I pushed my way past him and ran right into a solid wall. Wait, it was a red-haired woman wearing a black pleather corset. *Yes, I could instantly tell it wasn't real leather. Hello? Something told me it wasn't because she cared about animals, either.*

"You're not a member," she snapped.

Another scream, accompanied by other grunts, groans and moans echoed up from the basement. By now the shrill noises had cut my patience pretty short. "I'm an officer of the law and am citing exigent circumstances to investigate an emergency situation." I tried to push past her but she grabbed my arm in an iron grip.

"You're what and inciting who?" she asked.

"Look, someone is screaming down there and if you're obstructing justice, you're an accessory to whatever is happening."

The woman just laughed. I managed to rip my elbow out of her clutches. Then I charged down the stairs throwing my full weight against the door at the bottom. To my surprise, it opened and I went flying into the room, skittering across a polished hardwood floor right on my Vera Wang. The man in black leather pants and a black leather mask who had opened the door, closed it behind me and latched it.

"Who the hell are you?" He stood with his hands on his hips. That's when I noticed a whip in his hand and a naked woman chained to the back wall— begging for more. She had some red welts on her back, thighs and butt that made me shudder. Through glass cubicles, I saw others engaged in various stages of S&M. One room housed three participants. It looked as if two women were sharing one naked guy, which meant that the one in the back must have been wearing a strap-on. Ick. In another glass cubicle a nude woman was bent over a pair of black leather pants, getting the paddling of her life. What in the world could she have done to deserve that?

Other rooms stood vacant and some had dark shades drawn, so it was impossible to tell if they were in use or not. What appeared to be cleaning supplies sat outside each of the rooms on a rolling cart, along with a fishbowl filled with foil packs. Condoms?

"What the hell is this place?" I shouted as I pushed myself up onto my white satin pumps and whirled around, taking in the entire scene. Manacles hung on concrete walls. An empty room on the other side with its door open sported what looked like a doctor's exam table. Another empty room held a brass bed with handcuffs on all four bedposts and a sofa pushed against the opposite wall. For viewing? More screwing? Eek. I didn't want to know.

At the front of the room stood a small stage occupied by an opulent chair and a man wearing black. Seated next to him was some kind of big dog, like a malamute. It stood as I stared. Bared teeth and a low growl reminded me of Wolfie. A wolf-dog. Just what I needed.

"Easy, Tundra," the man said in a low, even voice. The animal relaxed and sat on his haunches.

Turning his attention to me the guy said, "Come here" in a gentle tone of voice, as if talking to a child. Something about him made me want to obey. I don't know if that was some kind of animal magnetism or what. Maybe it was because he looked like sex on a stick or more accurately sex on a throne.

"I'm sorry, sir," said the guy in the mask. "I don't know who she is or how she got in here."

The guy he called "sir" seemed to be the leader so I figured it wouldn't be a bad idea to talk to him. I approached the stage, cautiously. The dog quivered and sniffed the air. The man simply said, "sit," and the obedient beast did. I almost did too. Or was that just my knees giving out from under me? He stood up tall and straight, probably a couple of inches over six feet, commanded his canine companion to stay and gracefully strolled to the stairs without taking his eyes off me. "And who might you be?" he asked in his silken voice as he approached.

"I might be a police officer." I jammed my hands on my hips trying to look tough. Actually with all the ruffles and lace I had to place my hands on my satin waistband but I leaned forward in my most intimidating stance.

He simply continued to stroll toward me. He halted about three feet away and looked me over, appraising my lovely outfit from the top of my veil to the tips of my satin shoes.

"I see," he said and smirked.

Trying to ignore the amused expression on his face, I lifted my chin. "Is this a BDSM club?" I asked, stupidly.

He smiled but didn't answer. Instead, he asked me his own questions. "This is a private club. Are you a guest? Did you receive an invitation?"

"Yeah. I heard someone screaming bloody murder. Since it sounded like someone needed immediate help, I invited myself. I even ran out on my own wedding to investigate. The noise led me here."

He slipped his hands into his pockets and adopted a more casual stance. "So you were doing your duty and putting your own desires aside. I admire that kind of dedication."

"Yeah, well, arresting you will be worth it."

"Me? What did I do?"

"You seem to be the one in charge here. Of course everyone in this room is under arrest."

He chuckled. "And how are we to be taken into custody?"

Unfortunately, I was stumped for an answer to that. I had no gun, no badge, no radio. What I did have was a serious case of poor impulse control. What was I thinking? Did I expect these people to take the handcuffs off the beds and put them on each other, then line up nicely at the door so I could march them across the street?

I blustered my way through. "This type of club condones assault, sodomy and a slew of other legal infractions. I'm betting you know that since it's completely concealed and you have bouncers at the door."

By now the man in the mask had sidled up next to me. "What should we do with her, sir?"

Before anyone had a chance to answer, I whirled

and aimed my white three-inch heel at his groin. My foot reverberated like it hit iron. In actuality, his big meaty hands had caught my shoe and stopped it just as it contacted something metal under the leather. *Uh-oh.*

He pushed my foot, trying to make me fall backward but I staggered and caught my balance. I didn't know how many times I could fall on my ass without tearing my would-be-outrageously-expensive-had-I-paid-retail garment. I'd decided to use that opportunity as the lucky break it was and dashed for the door. I managed to get to it and turn the deadbolt just in time to run into the pair who had been at the top of the stairs. The woman pushed me backward and this time I fell flat on my ass.

"Hey! Watch it. I paid fourteen hundred dollars for this designer dress." I didn't but I could have.

She turned to the guy in the bra and barked, "Stay upstairs, Sunny. I'll find out what's going on." Then she closed the door and relocked it.

The Amazon woman reached over and hauled me to my feet. I stood and brushed off my dress in an effort to look dignified.

The well-dressed man people called "sir" strolled toward us and said, "So far, Juliet, all we've been able to ascertain is that she's a police officer who thinks this might be an illegal BDSM club and apparently she got past you at the front door."

Juliet? This woman with the build and finesse of a Mack truck was named Juliet?

"I'm sorry, sir. It's my fault. I'll kick her out." The woman grabbed my arm and began to drag me toward the door

"No," Sir said, "we can't let her leave."

"Can't let me leave? Are you crazy? It's not like you can adopt me or convert me to your way of life and it's highly unlikely you'll get away with murder. Besides, there's a synagogue full of folks wondering where I am as we speak. Plus, do you know who I am?"

"No." He looked me up and down. "Should I?"

"I'm Faith Daniels, daughter of Saul Daniels." When his expression didn't change, I continued. "The furniture king?"

"Ah, I see. So we have the privilege of being arrested by a princess."

"A Jewish American princess by the looks of it," Juliet chimed in.

I didn't care how strong the bitch was or how many manicured fingernails I could break—she was going down. I reached her in two short strides and threw a punch with as much power as I had behind it.

I must have caught her just right because the weeble wobbled and she *did* fall down—with a solid thud. I'm surprised the hardwood floor didn't crack—and the sub-floor. She was temporarily neutralized, but I heard a low, menacing but sexy voice behind me say, "Restrain our guest."

Chapter One and a Half
Dorian's take on the situation

It started out as a normal early evening at the BDSM club. A few early clients, a few screams of erotic pain, a grunt or two of gagged ecstasy.

So why did I have to go and wish for something different? Something new? And in what sick and twisted world did that mean a blonde bombshell who thinks she's Chick Norris?

A little change meant a new toy, be it plastic or a pussy with a unique talent, or watching a new client with a monster cock determined to invade and conquer. Instead, I get a hot blonde cop in a wedding dress. Jesus.

Still, I had to admit I was curious to see how she was going to play this out. I also wasn't one hundred percent sure this wasn't a put-on once she said she was a cop. If I had a dollar for every time a stripper in a cop uniform was sent over... Well, let's just say the wedding dress could be a new twist on an old joke.

I got to work, tuning out the protests and threats

of bodily harm as Guy and I systematically removed both dress and shoes, then tied the princess up. I would have gagged her too but damned if those protests and threats didn't make my cock stir.

One look at Juliet still flopping around on the floor trying to catch her breath cured me of that pleasure. I'd played side-by-side with many a Dominatrix and found them to be sexy as hell. Juliet did nothing for me. I sighed and forced myself to go back into business mode. First things first and no way was I leaving Juliet alone with blondie.

"Guy, I need you to throw on some street clothes and figure out what's going on in front of the temple. If anyone is going to come looking for her, I want plenty of warning. I also need to know when the coast is clear for us to move her."

"Aw, boss, you know how difficult it is to get the codpiece back on when I'm already hard!"

"Then have a sub blow you when you get back."

Geez, did I have to think of everything? I looked down to find the Princess Bride glaring at me and I glared right back. I wasn't the one who had invaded her space, dammit! I wonder how she would feel about being tied to the bedposts of one of Daddy's special deals I picked up last month. Truth be told, it wasn't that impressive a bed. The one from a competitor had lasted two months before it began to give from the chafing of restrained subs.

"I'm gonna kill that bitch!" Juliet yelled.

I stopped her with a snarl, trained as she was to obey me. It didn't matter if she was master or sub—I ruled here. Bottom line, I sign her paycheck, and paid gigs were a rarity in this business. "We have clients. Go do your job while I wait for Guy."

Juliet did love her job. It was all of thirty seconds before I heard the swish of the knotted cat-o-nine, but the gasp of shock didn't come from the recipient. No, Harold the banker clearly enjoyed being bent over the padded sawhorse for his Mistress' touch.

The gasp came from the bundle of blonde joy that had dropped on my doorstep and damned if the sound didn't hold more than a smidgen of arousal.

It wasn't long before Guy came back, just as Juliet finished off Harold. The latter's red ass danced and shuddered for the audience that had gathered, though no one dared to block my view. Or the princess's. I knew because I was watching her. I couldn't believe it but the idea of her getting wet was actually more exciting than the show itself.

There wasn't any time to dwell on that now. Guy and I secured her to the wall in the recovery room, then dragged Juliet away to put my plan into motion.

Chapter Two
Faith's story continued…

Chained to the wall next to the girl with the welts, I heard Dorian and the others as they discussed my fate. I wanted to ask poor welt-girl what the hell she was doing there but I was kind of afraid of the answer. Oh, yes. I'd discovered his name was Dorian when I asked him who the hell he thought he was to keep me there and called him "sir" in my snidest tone of voice.

Juliet was all for weighting my ankles and tossing me into the river. Then she snorted, "No, that won't work. I think witches float."

The other guy sounded pensive as he said, "Dr. Martin Luther King said something like, 'Faith is taking the first step even when you can't see the entire staircase.' I vote for pushing her down the stairs."

The three of them shared a maniacal laugh at my expense. How infuriating.

It seemed that Dorian knew someone who could erase people's memories. He had a nightclub act or something. He wanted to take me home with him and asked Guy to contact the guy—I mean, the other guy, the hypnotist. Guy was the name of the man in the mask. I wondered how long he'd have to keep me there before that happened. After that, I'd probably look like just another "runaway bride."

Turning to the girl next to me, I noticed she hung there just as peacefully as if she were holding a ladder for someone. "So, what's a nice girl like you doing in a place like this?"

She whispered, "I'm not allowed to talk to the other guests."

Not allowed to talk? Was she kidding me? She had been screaming her head off ten minutes ago. I didn't want to get her into trouble so I turned my attention to the strange trio deciding my fate.

"It's a good thing only a few people have arrived," Guy said.

Dorian glanced around the club at the other members looking on. "It's still early."

"Well, we need to get her out of here before she sees some of our better known members," Juliet added. "Are you sure you want to take her home with you?"

"Yes. You and Guy can handle the place tonight. I think it's best if I take care of things since I seem to be the only one who doesn't want to kill her."

Guy folded his arms. "Like you said, sir, it's still early."

He chuckled. "Contact Luciano's club in Atlantic City, then send him to my house."

Hey, did I mention they'd removed my gorgeous white gown? Yeah. Here I dangled in my white corset and white stockings after yelling about how they were going to pay for dry cleaning. Oh and they took my high heels too. That was a shame since they were the only makeshift weapons I had. Well, those and my teeth but I was saving my jaws for whichever unlucky slob came to release me. I hoped it would be one of the guys because then I could bite and distract while my knee found a groin.

Juliet frowned and stormed toward me. Damn. *Looks like she lost the coin toss.*

She paused, pulled a little rubber ball and a black kerchief out of her pocket and held them up. "I assume you don't want to listen to her gripe and whine all the way home, sir?"

"That would be correct," Dorian said.

"And should I shackle her so she can't run away or knee you in the groin?"

"Yes, Juliet. Very thoughtful of you."

Then an evil smile appeared on her ugly mug and she approached with more confidence. Well, it looked like I was going somewhere against my will unless I could catch another lucky break. At least I was going with the young stud who didn't encase himself in cheap plastic and want to kill me.

"Open wide," she said, cruelly.

"Why? So I can suck your cock?"

She jammed the ball between my teeth and I tried to bite her fingers. Sadly, I missed but at least the ball didn't go right past my teeth and down my gullet. I was probably the only one there who knew CPR.

"Now, is that appropriate language for a virginal bride?"

I could do nothing but grunt my assent. I wasn't a virgin but my mother didn't know that when she picked out my dress. Nobody could do denial like my mother.

I kept looking for opportunities to escape or at least go down fighting. I just needed some kind of vindication. At least that way, if I inflicted damage on these pricks in the scuffle, my fellow cops would nod at my funeral and say, "Yup, she was brave to the end. She died with honor."

Sorry, I didn't mean to get all morbid on you. My life didn't flash before my eyes or anything. It's just that the freakishly strong dominatrix made sure I was good and helpless. Her crowning achievement was to slip a black bag over my head, which she duct taped around my neck.

"Ah, yes. Silence is golden but duct tape is silver."

Trying to babble anything around the ball just led to more humiliation, so I gave up trying to voice my displeasure. Besides, it added to the unflattering drool leaking around the ball. If my mom could see me now, she'd shit.

When I was good and hog-tied, someone, I assume it was Dorian—strong arms, scratchy material—lifted me effortlessly. Show off. I had one more hair-brained scheme that might work. Once I could assume I was outside and on my way to his car, I might be able to wriggle and squeal and make enough of a ruckus to attract the attention of someone who happened to be walking by the opposite end of the alley right at that moment. Hey, it *could* work.

Maybe I'd buy a little time if I wiggled out of his grasp, hit the ground and squirmed away… Oh hell. I was caught. Might as well begin cooperating until he let his guard down.

They teach us that in Hostage 101. Well, okay, it's

not really called Hostage 101. It's called Hostage Negotiations but regular town cops never get to do the important stuff. We get to watch while SWAT and the feds come in and take over. Yawn.

So it was time to cooperate and just lie in those strong arms, picturing Mr. Luscious carrying me to his car, which would, of course, be a black Mercedes or Lexus. Even wrapped in a blanket as I was now, his heat penetrated my skin and for some stupid reason it relaxed me.

The engine purred. I had been laid horizontal in the back seat, surprisingly gently. Now there was nothing to do but listen for sounds of the railroad, the ocean or school children to figure out where I was. Unfortunately, with my luck I would probably hear all three at the same time and that would be as confusing as hell.

I tried to estimate the time we took to get to our destination. It may have been half an hour and the traffic noise was fairly light for a Friday evening. I guessed we were probably driving out of the suburban area into the country somewhere. Maybe he knew of some smelly, abandoned barn where he could store me. Oh, goody.

Toward the end of our ride, I sensed a change in elevation…hills or mountains since I was leaning into the back of the seat with more pressure. Okay maybe it was a mountain cabin hideaway. I hoped for one of those nifty hunting cabins with guns hung on the walls. Yeah, that would be neat. But I doubted anyone could be that dumb.

Dorian hadn't said a word. There was little reason to. I was unable to answer and completely at his mercy. I listened for sounds of crunching gravel or something to indicate that we were close to the destination. There seemed to be very little sound at all. A few birds chirping or maybe they were cicadas—I was never very good at nature sciences.

Finally we glided smoothly to a stop. The back door opened a moment after the front door opened and closed. So I assumed it was Dorian who was lifting me up again and carrying me.

After the sound of a click and whoosh of a door opening and closing, I heard some short beeps. An alarm system. Well I guessed I'd be safe and secure. Snort.

He gently laid me supine on another yielding surface and then sat me up. I was unbelievably relieved when he removed the duct tape and lifted the smothering bag off my head. Never mind that my hair crackled with static electricity and I probably looked like Bill the cat, I could breathe again. Now he stood before me, hands on hips, with a stern expression on his handsome face. No I wasn't not having Stockholm Syndrome or anything. He was still a prick—just a devilishly good-looking one.

"Now if I take the ball out of your mouth are you going to yell, spit or verbally abuse me? In other words, will I just have to put it back where it was?"

I shook my head.

"Promise?"

I nodded.

He took the ball out of my mouth and just stood there, waiting for me to scream or harass him. I didn't. I simply asked for a glass of water. He hesitated, probably wondering what I was planning to do with it other than refresh myself.

"I won't spit it in your face. I'm just hot, thirsty

and tired. And can you please take this stupid blanket off me? Right now my modesty is the least of my problems."

A slow, gleaming grin crept across his face.

* * * * *

I sat at Dorian's ten-foot-long, shiny, granite breakfast bar sipping a glass of water through a straw. That sounds a lot more casual than it actually was. The bar had one of those long cylindrical footrests, a three-inch diameter steel pipe bolted to the floor—with my ankles shackled to it. I used the straw since I couldn't hold a glass with my hands cuffed behind my corseted back.

Dorian sipped his glass of orange juice with no impediments and looked me over a little too thoroughly. "I guess you didn't really want to get married today."

"Sure I did."

"So why did you run out on your fiancé?" he asked.

"I told you. I heard screams."

"How? You must have been in the alley near the back door to hear anything at all. In fact, it's never come to my attention that our reinforced steel doors and concrete walls weren't completely soundproof."

"Sorry. Someone should have told you."

A half smile played across his sexy lips. They were still plump, something I didn't see on any men but the youngest rookies. How old did you have to be to run a BDSM club, anyway? It just seemed like a job that needed an age limit.

Trying to look way more casual than I felt, I cocked my head to one side. "Now, can I ask you a question?"

"You can ask. I may not answer."

"How old are you?"

He set his glass in the perfectly clean stainless steel sink. "Why?"

"I don't know, I'm just curious. Looking at you, I'd guess early twenties, yet you own a very—ahem—adult club and this huge, luxurious home. Oh and please satisfy my curiosity about the car. German or American?"

Did I forget to mention his home could have jumped off the pages of a contemporary interior design magazine and sat atop a small mountain all by itself? Huge floor to ceiling glass windows revealed twinkling lights of a town below and little else.

"That's more than one question." He slipped his hands in the pockets of his black tweed pants. It was hard to read his expression. He didn't seem annoyed or amused. To be honest, he seemed bored. Was I really such poor company?

"Okay, I'm more curious about your age. The car can wait until I see it again—after you wipe my memory, I imagine."

He raised his eyebrows. "You heard us talking?"

"Yeah. Thanks for refusing to let the other two kill me."

He shrugged. Strolling around the counter, gaze on the floor, he said, "I'm twenty-eight. Just." Then he looked up at me and appeared to study my face. "And you? I'd guess you're thirty? Maybe thirty-two?"

I wanted to kiss him but I'd never tell him that. He might take it the wrong way. "I'm thirty-eight. Ten years your senior."

He simply nodded and sat on the stool next to me. Too bad. I'd hoped for an expression of shock.

Maybe then I would have kissed him. Not now, though. He blew it by accepting reality far too well.

"So how did you get into the, um, entertainment business," I asked, trying to be tactful.

"Are you hungry?"

By this time I brilliantly deduced he didn't want to tell me anything about his business. His question was an obvious attempt to change the subject. Just then, my stomach answered for me. *Grrrooowwwl.*

I shrugged. "I could eat. By the way, where's your dog?"

"Tundra's not my dog. She belongs to the club."

Part of me was horrified. That had to be a bad environment for such a beautiful animal. "She lives there? Who takes care of her?"

"Would you like some scrambled eggs?"

I sighed. "I guess there's no hope of having the chicken cordon bleu the caterer boasted was the best on the eastern seaboard?"

"I guess not."

"Okay. Scrambled eggs sound yummy." I wondered if he was going to feed them to me or expect me to stick my face in the plate and lap them up like Tundra. "Is there any chance you'd take these cuffs off so I can eat? I promise I won't try to escape."

He chuckled. "I'm not worried about you escaping. The house is locked electronically. Without the code, no one is getting in or out. Even a battering ram won't shatter the glass."

Hmm… I wondered how he knew that. Did he test it with medieval weaponry? "So you think I'm going to hurt you or something? What could a little lady like me do? Try to find a weapon and force you to give me the code?"

"Not if you know what's good for you."

"Fine. Then can I please have my hands back to feed myself? It's not like I'm going to stab you with a fork."

He stared at me intently, then unlocked my handcuffs. "Fine but since you thought about it, you'll be using a plastic spoon."

Fuck.

A few minutes later as I was scarfing down some damn good scrambled eggs and toast, I heard a purr.

"Do you have a cat?"

"A cat?" He repeated. "No. Why?"

"I hear purring. It's getting louder. I think it's outside. Maybe you have a tiger, roaming the grounds for protection?"

He cocked his head, looked at me strangely and furrowed his brow until lights radiated through the windows and splashed against the back wall."

"Oh, my bad," I said. "It's a truck, not a tiger."

"You're a very odd girl." As he left the kitchen, he said, "I'll be back in a minute."

"Okay, I'll be right here."

He tossed a look of amusement over his shoulder.

This must be the mind-wiping magician. Just as well. The sooner this nightmare ended, the better. If I failed in my duty as a police officer, at least I'd never know it. My main worry, however, wasn't my job. What the hell was I going to tell my mother?

After a series of beeps, presumably from Dorian disarming the alarm system, I heard Guy's voice. "Sorry, sir. He's not there anymore. Seems like he got a promotion or something. Some big hotel gave him a gig in Vegas."

"Shit."

"May I come in to use the head before I go back to the club?"

"Of course and I have another request while you're here."

A few minutes later the two men entered the kitchen. Dorian held a digital camera and handed it to Guy. "I want you to take a couple of pictures of my ladylove and me."

Ladylove huh? This was news to me.

Guy chuckled. "Talk about fast work! How the hell did that happen?"

Dorian strolled over to me and put an arm around my shoulder. "It didn't but I need a couple of pictures to make it look like she's mine in case the runaway bride disappears while we're in Vegas."

"We're going to Vegas?" Wow, talk about an opportunity. Maybe I *could* escape, notify the cops and play some slots while they closed down the torture chamber.

"Of course she'll need some new clothes. I can't very well take her out like this, such a pity. Can you ask Juliet to pick some up and have them waiting in my office?"

I gasped. They both stared at me. "Are you sure you want Juliet shopping for my clothes? I mean, I don't think we have the same taste by any stretch of the imagination."

Dorian gave me a look that brooked no argument. "What size?"

Guy folded his arms. "For your information, Juliet's a pretty successful New York designer."

Dorian rolled his amber brown eyes. "Oh great, another piece of information we'll have to erase from her mind."

A dominatrix designer in fake leather. Now I've heard everything. "Hey, I won't say a thing if she gets me some nice clothes. I'm a size ten at the cheap stores, size six or eight at the really good ones."

They eyed me strangely.

"It's a thing. She'll understand. I prefer neutrals in the warm color palettes with maybe one pop of bright color. I look best in greens and blues sometimes red, depending on the—"

Guy shook his head. "I'm not going to remember all that. You'll get what she gives you. Now let's take these pictures so I can get out of here."

Dorian placed a possessive arm around me and squeezed as I sat on the stool helpless to move out of the way.

"Say cheese, darling."

I did my best to screw up my face so I looked miserable, or at least uncooperative.

Guy shook his head. "She's making ugly faces, sir."

Dorian grabbed my head in both hands. One cupped the back of my skull and the other held my jaw. He pulled my lips to his in a crushing kiss. Actually that was just the start of the kiss. This was the kind of kiss a girl dreams about but thinks she'll never have in her lifetime. A toe-curling, earth-shaking, multiple-orgasm-promising kiss that leaves you boneless. Did I kiss him back? Hell, yeah!

After a couple of shots of the two of us together, Dorian took the camera and snapped a couple of close-ups of me. I was tempted to push out my lower lip to show how badly I had been treated but he would've made me do it over again until they came out right.

Then he handed the camera to Guy. "Take this to the office, download it to my computer and be sure that the date is on them. Then print out a copy of each and I'll pick them up on our way to the airport." He gave me a meaningful look and turned his attention back to Guy as he added, "If I ask you to email them, be sure these pictures get to our friends in low places."

"Yes, sir."

"I'll let you out."

Well that was an interesting turn of events. Apparently, I'd be posing as Sir Dorian's wife. I wondered if that made me Lady Dorian? I had to hope and pray that these pictures never fell into the hands of the enemy—my mother. Then I'd really be dead.

After hearing the numerous beeps of the alarm system and his return to the kitchen, he seemed almost pleased. I'd have thought he'd be pissed off but no. A lazy look of secret satisfaction bent one side of his lips and then spread to the other.

"It looks like you'll be spending the night with me," he said.

Okay, so now I knew why he was smiling. "You expect me to sleep with you, don't you? Well, that isn't going to happen. Oh, no. No way."

"You don't have much say in the matter."

Chapter Two and a Half
Dorian saw it this way

After driving all over town for half an hour, I finally felt comfortable enough to head straight for my house in the hills above the city. It was normally a ten-minute ride from work but that didn't include needing to disorient a near-naked, firmly trussed, crap-she-really-is-a-police officer in my backseat. Go figure.

Funny thing was, I'd been finding myself asking more and more lately, what was "normal"? My life as a successful BDSM club owner ensured every day was filled with whips and chains and the accompanying groans of pleasured pain that filled my...bank account. Yes, bank account. Somewhere along the way, the financial success of the club had begun to excite me more than making a female sub suck my cock while having her ass striped.

Yet here I was, getting off on a kinky scenario that didn't involve pain, just an unwilling bride. It didn't even have anything to do with the fact that she'd been hog-tied and ball-gagged, which from what I understood fit more with the groom's fantasy *after* twenty years of marriage. Or maybe ten years in Bridezilla's case.

It didn't matter. What had me hard was that I wasn't the groom. Shit. If I'd figured that part out back at the club, I'd have brought that silk and lace monstrosity of a dress with us. It was definitely too late for that one. No doubt Juliet had shredded it into a thousand doilies by the time I'd left the parking lot. Vindictive bitch. Then again, that's what made her a valued employee.

But I didn't want to think about Juliet earning the employee of the month cake right then, though it had been funny how she'd simply taken the buttercream confection from Guy last month, then eaten it right in front of him. Hey, what was I supposed to do about it? The stronger Dom took the cake. If I'd wanted the damn thing, I would have taken it from her. Besides, Guy got more reward out of having it taken away and being teased with it, valued switch that he was. His dual preferences kept the payroll down.

Such was my life. Day in, day out, always the same games. Until now. The princess-bride-in-bondage was definitely a new one, though the cop part wasn't. I'd paddled two sergeants and a captain the week before, then walked away to finish the monthly budget without needing to get off.

I knew that wasn't going to be the case tonight, even before I pulled up to my place and prepared to carry the bride over the threshold. The grin on my face wasn't the only thing growing wider and I knew one way or another, I wouldn't end the night finessing numbers.

The alarm system gave its lock-down beeps before I was comfortable putting my precious bundle down on the leather couch. She had been so quiet that I actually considered leaving her there like that but then I remembered that was due to the ball-gag, not by choice. Still…I found myself wincing as I removed the hood and sure enough, her eyes were spitting fire right at me. It scorched me all right but probably not the way she'd intended. I made her promise to cooperate before I unlatched the gag but I should have known it wouldn't be enough.

There was a big difference between cooperating and demanding. In fact, I found out pretty quickly that it was possible to do both at the same time. I couldn't help thinking that if anyone had ever stolen *her* cake, they'd get to eat it all right. Their face would be planted in it.

Christ, I wanted to fuck her. Fuck her hard, fuck her now. I found myself wondering how long it had been since I'd had vanilla sex, since I'd simply lost myself in the soft skin and delicate tastes and scents of the female body. Too long. Long enough for me to get hard and stay hard from the moment Faith Daniels barreled into my life.

Long enough to make the situation a true moral dilemma. I couldn't let word of my boredom get out any more than I could let Bridezilla back out into the wild without erasing her memory of me and my club. And as long as I had to have it erased, it seemed to me we could have a little fun together. I mean, what bride wouldn't want to get laid on her wedding night?

Yep, sounded perfectly rational to me.

Except I imagined the hypnotist was already on his way. Great. I set her up at the kitchen counter instead and it took all of five minutes for me to again wish I'd never taken the damn gag out. The woman was determined to get as much information out of me as she could, probably hoping she'd retain some bit of info to bust me with later. And she seemed to have some kind of supersonic hearing thing going on that was more than a little freaky.

I was almost relieved when Guy got there, until I found out that Plan A had bit the dust and I had to create Plan B on the fly. Then I kissed Faith for the first time and I realized having to go to Plan B wasn't a bad thing. Oh yeah. From the way she kissed me back, there was a damn good chance we'd be doing the honeymoon happy dance before the night ended.

Chapter Three
Faith tried formulating a plan…

Because I was shackled, the wrong man carried me down the hall on my wedding night. The irony was not lost on me. By this time, I had formulated a new escape plan. I'd try to seduce him. If he would leave me unshackled so I could—ahem—spread my legs, I might be able to run.

The only weapons I had at the moment were my teeth and I could think of only one way to disable him long enough to find a real weapon. The old Lorena Bobbitt trick but could I do it? My stomach twisted at the horrible thought. I really wasn't up for blood sausage in my mouth. But if it came down to my own survival, I'd have to do something. He must have some sort of gun for self-defense. If not, I'd seen some dandy knives in the kitchen.

As he carried me over the threshold to his bedroom, I gazed up at him. His eyes seemed to darken with lust as he met my stare. He set me on my feet and turned me around to face the bed, already equipped with leather restraints on each corner. What a freak.

"Sit."

"You really can trust me at this point, you know. I don't want to be tied up. After all, you've made it clear there's no escape." I ran a finger across his lips down his chin and over his chest. In my sexiest whisper I said, "We could have more fun that way, don't you think?"

His eyebrows arched. "Are you saying you'll cooperate if I want to fool around?"

"Sure why not? You're a handsome guy and I was planning to have sex tonight anyway."

"What makes you think I was planning on it?" He sat me down on the bed took my left hand and had the restraint around my wrist in seconds, even though I twisted and pulled away, frantically.

"Hey! I'm not one of your sex slaves. I'm ready and willing. You don't need to do this whole bondage thing with me."

"My bed, my rules."

"Fine, let's go to my place, then." I yanked on the restraint, trying to loosen it before he could fasten the lock. He just pulled it tighter and I yelped in pain. I began to call him every name in the book until he reminded me that I could be gagged again too. Oops, that wouldn't work in my favor at all. He didn't seem angry or raise his voice. He simply spoke to me as if explaining a logical mathematical equation in a lecture hall.

"I'm sorry," I said and tried to look contrite. I was supposed to be seducing him and maybe I could still get him to take the restraints off if I played nice. I had decided I couldn't use my teeth on his cock. That was just too horribly peculiar and thinking about it made me throw up in my mouth a little bit. But considering how much my wrist hurt, I just might have to reconsider.

"It won't hurt at all if you cooperate. Now, am I going to be able to take off the shackles without your kicking me?"

I didn't know much about BDSM but I kind of thought part of the turn-on for the Dominant was to push people around and rough them up. He was actually being kind of nice under the circumstances. "Yes, Dorian. Please, I promise I won't kick you."

That brought a Cheshire cat smile to his lips if ever I saw one.

As he unlocked the chains I noted which key he used in case I wound up in leg irons again. I'd also have to make a mental note of where he put them. "If you leave me unbound, I could make you feel good too." When he scrutinized me, I winked. Now if that didn't look stupidly obvious I don't know what did.

To my surprise, he left my legs free. As he slipped the keys into his left pocket, I realized he was going to immobilize only one wrist and that was all. Sitting next to me on the bed, he unfastened one of my garters and carefully rolled the white hose down my leg and off my foot. Then the other one. Shaking them out, he draped each one over an antique chair. I hoped it wasn't loaded with splinters. I couldn't believe how well they'd held up already but might as well not tempt fate. "Do you think you could rinse those out and hang them over the shower rod?"

He didn't answer or make any move to care for my expensive stockings. "Do you want to sleep in this?" he asked, with a sweep of his hand over my corset.

Ashlyn Chase & Dalton Diaz

Now what? Do I let him see my saggy breasts and hope it turns him on? As I hesitated, he unclasped his belt buckle, unzipped his black dress pants and let them fall to the floor.

"Ah...don't go to any trouble. I can sleep like this."

Then he tossed his pants out the door and down the hallway. "Just in case you get any ideas about knocking me out and dragging the bed over to get the keys."

"Huh. I never thought of that."

"I'm surprised."

"Why? Does it look like I'm trying to escape?" I asked, innocently.

"No but I'm not letting my guard down. Women have done some pretty creative things to get away from me."

Eek. That didn't sound good. Then one side of his mouth rose and I realized he was joking. He *was* joking wasn't he? Okay, I hoped he was joking.

He held my gaze as he shed the rest of his clothes.

Oh, Mama! The man was built. Even more intriguing was his all-over tan. His cock, only half aroused, promised to be impressive and I caught myself gaping at it, looking forward to stroking his hard-on. Thank God he was circumcised. I'd never learned what to do with a foreskin and being Jewish, I doubted I'd ever need to know.

His lips twitched in amusement. "You're a naughty girl, aren't you? Funny, I had you pegged for a prude."

Indignant at the insulting near-truth, I bristled. "I'm not a prude." But my vagina was probably full of cobwebs.

He raised an eyebrow.

"I've had my share of experience but I'm sure it pales in comparison to yours." There. I hoped that would stroke his male ego.

"Perhaps you haven't found a skilled lover—yet."

Oh, puleeease. Now who was being obvious? Should I feel ashamed of what I was about to do? Undoubtedly—even though it was part of the escape plan. So why didn't I?

He dimmed the lights with one of those dimmer switches. It looked like he was prepared for anything. He slid in next to me and—*Oh my God, protection!*

"Do you have a condom?"

"Do I need one?"

Shit. I can't believe I just assumed and he didn't... My face heated. "Well, you never know. I mean—you might or you might not. I guess it all depends. I thought you...but if you didn't..." I must have been blushing furiously. The curse of being blonde. Well, one of two curses and I had apparently demonstrated both.

"I like a woman who can still blush." He rose from the bed and retrieved a box from his dresser drawer. I didn't know whether to be relieved or terrified.

My seduction seemed to be working and I hadn't even tried. Maybe subconsciously... No, that couldn't be true. I mean, I know he's tall, dark and as sexy as sin but my libido wasn't that out of control, was it? No, I knew exactly what I was doing—or so I told myself.

Then he set the box on the bedside table and stroked my cheek with the back of his fingers. Lying down, facing me, he tipped my chin toward him and stared into my eyes. Their dark intensity promised a few pages for my secret memoirs. I hadn't planned to write any but after tonight, I might need to.

"What shall we do, Faith?"

Screw like rabbits? Yeah, I was in control, all right. I was praying that he'd free my wrist soon and after we were done, I could take my best shot at his tender groin.

"If you'll just let me have my other hand, I can do some marvelous things."

He shook his head. "Clearly, I'm not going to do that. Perhaps I can begin while you think of creative uses for your one hand, thighs and feet."

Feet? He wants me to use my feet? Don't tell me he has a foot fetish too. I wanted to squirm away from him but just then he pulled me forward and held me in his iron grip. His lips clamped down on mine and he swiftly injected his tongue into my mouth as I tried to gasp, creating a luscious vacuum instead.

He pushed me onto my back and it only took another minute of passionate kissing before my one free hand decided on its own to caress and squeeze his ass. Meanwhile my feet were busy twining around his legs. He pulled loose, quickly unlaced the corset and dove for my breasts.

I had never had my breasts devoured before. Licked and sucked, sure but not like this. He sensitized my nipples with a quick bite and then practically hoovered them down his throat. Good God! Who knew saggy breasts could turn a man on like that? Certainly not my mother. Of course, she probably hadn't had sex since my conception.

I arched off the mattress and moaned in sheer bliss. Fluttery sensations made their way from my breasts to my viscera. I thought I might come with no more stimulation than that. And then he added his hands to the equation, fondling me everywhere.

Maybe he was right. Maybe I just hadn't met a skilled lover—until now. As he kissed his way down to my navel, he continued feeling me up, down and all around. My head swirled, my nerve endings popped and I gave myself over to his dominance, for clearly that was what we both wanted.

As he removed my panties with his teeth, he blew his hot breath over my mons and I shivered. "It's good, isn't it? And it's going to get even better."

His tongue swept the inside of my thigh and I thought I was going to jump off the bed. Not to worry, I thought. My little leather tether will keep me safe from hitting the ceiling.

Once I was separated from my underwear, he spread my labia and ran his tongue over all the ridges, carefully avoiding the top of the hill.

"You want me, don't you? You want me as much as I want you." He plunged two stiffened fingers inside and I cried out.

"So wet, hot and tight. I'm going to enjoy fucking you."

Damn. I wanted to squirm until I made contact, clit to tongue. I knew if I did that though, he'd just avoid it even longer. I was beginning to catch on to his game. If I wanted to get my way at any point in time, I'd have to make sure he thought it was his idea. Great. I'd finally learned how to be assertive and I find a guy who I have to manipulate.

At last, he lapped my clit with a vengeance. In my wildest imagination I never expected an orgasm could overwhelm me like that. It wasn't like the usual slow build up to a climax. Not like climbing a mountain, then jumping off. It was more like being at the Grand Canyon and jumping in, hitting every rippling air pocket all the way down before landing in the Colorado River with a splash. I guess with Vegas on the brain, I had to use a regional metaphor.

Gasping and panting, unable to move, except for my chest heaving, I lay like Gumby ready to be molded into whatever shape Dorian wanted me. And as usual, he knew exactly what he wanted. He retrieved a condom from the box on the nightstand, ripped it open and watched me like a predator as he rolled it on. I guess he'd decided not to take a chance on my teeth. I didn't have the strength to bite anyway.

He pushed my legs open and positioned himself between them.

"I'm not crazy about the missionary position but it seems like the best choice at the moment."

I was still breathless, so the only agreement I could utter came out like a weak, "Uh-huh."

I had expected him to take me savagely, ramming his rod all the way in, riding me like a bucking bronco. Instead he entered me gently, almost reverently and paused a moment to kiss me. Just as soon as I thought I had him figured out, he surprised me again.

He began to move, slowly. "I'll bet the guys you've been with were light on the foreplay and only hot and heavy while fucking."

How did he know? Again, I uttered my only coherent response. "Uh-huh."

He smiled and pushed my damp hair away from my face. "You see? You've never been loved properly. There's a difference, isn't there?"

"Big difference." Oh good. Words. I could make words again. Maybe I could thrust my hips to meet his instead of lying here like a boneless rag doll.

As I moved with him in a sultry rhythm, I thought I saw his eyes glow. Did all men look like that in the throes of passion? I couldn't remember seeing anyone's eyes as they made love to me before. The room was usually dark for one thing and their faces were usually buried somewhere in the pillow beside my head. Of course, my eyes were closed more often than not.

I didn't want to close my eyes. I wanted to watch the sensations wash over Dorian. He reared back and took in a sharp breath sporadically but most of the time, he held my gaze and undulated with me. Occasionally, he leaned down to plant tiny kisses along my jaw, neck and ear. Anyone watching us would have thought we were very much in love—except for the one restraint that whispered, "I totally don't trust you."

After a lengthy, gentle fucking, Dorian said, "I'm getting close," and increased his pace.

I'd have said, "Go for it," or something equally romantic but I couldn't break the spell he had me under. Along with a faster thrust, he also pushed harder and deeper into my goodies. Instinctively, I knew that if I tipped my lower body at just the right angle, my clit would make contact with his pelvis. I did and wowza, we were off to the races!

I felt my peak building fast. I hung on one-handed and met him thrust for thrust. Pounding now, his face contorted. He apparently had no problem with me watching him climax because he stayed propped up on his elbows all the way there. At the moment in question, his eyes scrunched shut and he looked like he was in pain. Actually, there was no question about it. He emitted some short grunts and spasmed, jerking into me repeatedly.

My orgasm followed immediately afterward, shaking and shattering me to my core. I screamed my release and thrashed beneath him. He continued to ride me until I couldn't move. Anymore of this and I'd be his willing sex slave forever.

Chapter Three and a Half

Dorian kisses the bride…everywhere

Showtime.

I carried the now willing bride into my bedroom, knowing I had to keep it cool. No way was I going to make the first move and have her blame me come morning. Not that I expected any remorse but there was no pleasing some people.

Besides, she wanted me. There was no mistaking the pure lust in her gaze… or the way she stiffened when I turned her to face the bed. Damn. What, was she going to go all princess on me because the bedroom set wasn't from Daddy's store? No, wait, she was staring at the restraints on the posts. Cool. *That* I could deal with.

I told her to sit and…whoa! Her response was to come on to me. It didn't take a genius to figure out her real agenda and I took it as fair warning. I didn't need any teeth marks on Mr. Happy, thank you very much. Still, I decided to let her loose except for one hand but I made her work for it like she'd earned it.

Hey, I knew how to do the dominant thing, all right? Only she shot back by asking me to wash and rinse her stockings. Damn, she was something else! What, I don't know, just...else. Different. Interesting.

There was no question that she wanted me. The woman damn near drooled when I took my clothes off. It took all the control I had to stay at half-mast like her eager scrutiny wasn't getting to me. When I couldn't take it another second, I hit the dimmer switch and, bingo! She asked if I had a condom. I still played it cool but I knew I had won. Faith Daniels was mine for the night.

I didn't give her much time to think after that. There wasn't much choice for me once we began, either. One kiss and I was ready to dive in full throttle but there were those very lush, very *real* breasts to conquer, those pointed nipples just begging to be attended to. Then that hot, wet pussy to taste. Oh yeah. Her tongue could hold venom but her pussy was pure candy. Her orgasm rolled in like a freight train and she exploded in my mouth, feeding me more and draining her into total submission. I could have gone on for another hour but the urge to thrust hard and deep was climbing and I needed to maintain control.

Shit, my hand actually shook as I rolled on the condom. I slowed down and took a deep breath to reign in my control so I could give her what I knew she needed. I just didn't expect to need it so much myself. Not like this, anyway. I'm not sure I could place the last time I did a woman slow and easy, let alone missionary. It was so long ago that it was as if this was my first time. And it felt pretty damn good.

Forget that. It was fucking heaven. I wanted it to

last all night but Christ, I was only human.

"I'm getting close," I tried to warn her, hoping she could slow it down somehow.

Instead, she tipped her hips so I went deeper with each thrust, clenching me internally like she was trying to keep me there at the deepest point. I kid you not, a fireball ignited at the base of my spine, shooting so hot and deep out my dick it's a wonder the condom held. I didn't think that moment could get any better when I felt her explode around me, heard her actually scream my name with pleasure.

Oh yeah. No pain, no toys necessary. It was all me.

Chapter Four
Faith recaps the next day

The next morning, even before I opened my eyes I awoke with a sinking feeling. This wasn't Bermuda, was it? If I rolled toward the middle of the bed, I wasn't going to see my new husband next to me, was I? And worse? I was *relieved*.

My parents would be crazy with worry by now. Nobody knew where I was, including me and I seemed to be all right with that. What was wrong with me?

I had enjoyed my night in Dorian's bed a little too much. I didn't even want to escape. Of course after all the evening gymnastics, even if I had managed to slip out of my one restraint, I'd probably have made it as far as the living room where I'd have collapsed on the couch and promptly fallen asleep, anyway.

He was already up. I heard sounds coming from the kitchen and recognized the smell of fried bacon. Yum. Fat, salt and calories. I would have refused it under normal circumstances but right then, I felt like

I could eat the whole pig with only a tiny pang of Jewish guilt. As much as I was looking forward to breakfast, I had to pee first—and badly.

"Dorian," I called. "I need to get up now."

I waited but it didn't sound like he was coming. I was beginning to do the dance. "Dorian!" I crossed my legs and squeezed. Still no response. "You'll understand that it's your fault if I pee the bed, right?" I yelled.

He dashed down the hall and around the corner. "Hold on." Diving into his pants pocket, he found the key and opened the lock to my leather restraint.

Whew, just in time. I jumped out of bed. "Are you letting me go by myself?"

"Why? Do you need my help?"

"Just point the way, pal, and hurry."

"My, aren't you bossy in the morning." He pointed across the hall.

"Yeah. It looks like we're both Dominants."

He snorted.

* * * * *

Over breakfast, I decided to ask him a few questions I'd had about the lifestyle for some time. I clearly didn't get it. What I especially didn't get was the appeal for the submissive.

Happily he was willing to explain it to me.

"The psychology of BDSM is simple and yet complex depending on the people involved. The basics are simple. When you're the submissive, you're giving control of everything you do or have done to you to someone else. They're to bring you pleasure and to break the mental walls that you've put up against allowing yourself to feel. But in the end, it's the submissive who is in control."

"Huh? How the heck does that work?"

"It's their boundaries, their tolerance that must be obeyed. When you have the right of choice taken from you…to be told how to please someone, shown how to please someone and be disciplined when you fail, it's a release from having to control and dictate everything in your other life."

"So you do have other lives? You folks could be walking around among us and we'd never know you were Dominant or submissive in your BDSM life?"

He chuckled. "Domination takes on many forms. That said, I will tell you that I'm not a typical Dom. Technically it's my right to punish, to push, to break down the barriers in the submissive and to get her to let me see her submission, to see her essence without any barriers. But by doing so, I have a responsibility to bring her pleasure, to bring her happiness and to protect her."

"Protect her from what?"

"A Dom needs to protect his subs from themselves and from himself if he has darker aspects. Yes, there are those who humiliate, whip, chain and otherwise treat their submissives in a manner you might find upsetting. But this is done with consent and with the thought that it's part of the breaking down process, part of a submissive accepting that she's owned. For the Dominant, it's a mental state of, 'I own you, I protect you, I will bring you fulfillment and happiness but I will not brook disobedience. I will not have you choosing what you want—I know what you need and will give it in time.'"

"Like hell you will."

He laughed. As I munched on the crisp bacon, feeling less and less guilty with every delicious bite, I tried to digest the information he had just given me. I still didn't get it.

"I still don't understand how the submissive is in control."

"I said she is *ultimately* in control. She willingly gives herself over. And I'm only using the word she for convenience since there are plenty of men who want to be dominated. Anyway, she needs to know she will always be safe and that she can make the action stop when it's looking like it will exceed her tolerance."

"Oh yeah, the safe word. I've heard of that. So what's yours?"

He chuckled and grinned, like I was a little girl he was about to pat on the head. "I don't have one because I don't need one. I'm the Dom, remember? But if the new sub doesn't have one, I might suggest *yellow* meaning caution and *red* meaning stop."

I nodded. "Hmmm… I might actually make sense of it eventually. So you said you're not typical as a Dom. What did you mean by that?"

"My domination is less strict than some out there but the results are quite enjoyable. I may deny or postpone eventual fulfillment, along with certain scenarios that allow me to control the release, what she gets and doesn't get but serious active discipline is saved for only the most major infractions."

I rolled my eyes. "So you get to say if she comes or not? If she's a good girl, you bring her to orgasm but don't if she displeases you? That sounds like a sexist pig to me."

He shook his head. "You forget. She has given herself over to me. She wants me to make the choice for her. Do you think you got what you deserved last night?"

"Damn right I did." I folded my arms and even though I could see his point, I didn't want him to know that.

He sighed. "What you got last night was what you expected. You didn't give yourself over to me to discipline. You did, however, give yourself over to me as a lover."

"What I got last night was a little more than I expected." I gave him my best sultry look, hoping he'd catch my drift. Hey, I was horny again. So sue me.

Either he didn't hear my seduction, or he ignored it. I didn't dare make any more of a pass than that. Since it wasn't his idea, he'd probably turn me down flat. Instead, he continued to explain some of the other aspects of BDSM I had never heard of.

"A switch is someone who can go from Dom to sub using the agreed upon word or who will remain in one function for a session if that's their desire. What's nice is that switches can get more work because of the fact that they can bend both ways." He shot me a wicked grin. "You might be able to pick up some extra cash that way."

"Oh, hardy har har." I wasn't going to fall for that obvious attempt to ruffle my feathers.

His expression turned serious. "Since you've vacillated between the two roles in the short time I've known you, you gave yourself away."

"Okay this conversation has officially become too weird for me. I guess that's a caution so I should say yellow light, right?"

A smug smile tugged at his lips but he didn't say anything in response. He simply stood, picked up our empty dishes and took them to the sink. "The maid will get those later."

"Naturally. I'd expect nothing less."

Chapter Four and a Half

Dorian, lost in thought the next morning

I was actually glad the hypnotist couldn't be found right away. After last night, there was no way in hell I was giving Faith back without fucking her again. Repeatedly.

As I was making breakfast the next morning, trying to ignore my morning wood so I could feed us first, I kept reliving her cry of ecstasy. My name tearing from her, sounding desperate for release. Then I realized she really was calling me from the bedroom and from the tone of it we were right back to the Princess and the pee. Not pea as in, "You should have bought the mattress from Daddy," but literally pee as in, "Uncuff me or I'll wet your bed." Never having been into the golden side of sex games, I hotfooted it down the hall and set her free.

She wasn't going to try to physically hurt me anymore but that mouth was still going to be the death of me. She asked about the BDSM lifestyle over breakfast and I tried to explain it to her but I could tell she didn't really get it. Her nipples were as hard as rocks through the shirt I'd given her, though. Seeing that, I took a chance and told her where I thought she'd fit into the mold but all that achieved was to end the conversation. It didn't matter because I already knew I was right. Even if her mind denied that she was the ultimate switch, her body told me otherwise.

Besides, it was time we were on our way to Vegas.

Chapter Five

You know sociopaths can be charming

I had apparently proved myself worthy of sitting in the front seat with no bag over my head. I also got to wear a pair of his sweat shorts, which puckered with the drawstring pulled tight enough to stay on my hips and a T-shirt that fit like a too-large mattress pad. At least the seduction was good for something. He couldn't provide me with shoes, though. Not really important since he'd handcuffed me to my leg irons, so running would not only look ridiculous but wouldn't take me very far, very fast.

He promised to let me sit upright as soon as we exited the highway since I wouldn't know if we had gone north or south or how many exits had passed but meanwhile, I was stooped over like a Neanderthal. Odd, since he was clearly the Neanderthal here—even if he did drive a Lexus.

Maybe if I engaged him in conversation, we could build some kind of relationship. I could gain more trust and therefore more freedom. "So, how did you get into BDSM, anyway?"

At first he said nothing. I thought maybe it was another one of those "the less you know the better" things, or my question was so stupid it didn't deserve an answer.

"I grew up in the lifestyle. My father was a top and my mother, his bottom."

I tried to shake the disturbing image that created in my head. "How do people like that raise children? Shouldn't social services have stepped in the minute you told your teacher that Daddy beat Mommy?"

"It wasn't like that. My parents didn't demonstrate the darker side of the lifestyle in front of us kids. They may have gone to a club when we thought they were going out to dinner and a movie but they were very loving and devoted to each other."

"Kids? You mean you have brothers and sisters?"

"Had. I had a younger brother. He was in the car with my parents when it slid off an icy mountain road. They were on their way to a ski resort in Vail. All three of them were killed."

"Oh. I'm sorry. That must have been awful."

He shrugged.

I felt bad but continued anyway. "So you have no family?"

"I have an aunt somewhere."

"That's it? One relative and you don't know where she is? That must be so lonely."

"We all have our crosses to bear."

His voice hadn't changed inflection, as if the fact that he was so alone didn't bring up any feelings at all. I knew better. He was just very practiced at shrouding his real feelings. That didn't mean they weren't there.

"Besides, the club provides me a family, of sorts."

A BDSM club substituting for family? I suddenly felt enormous pity for this guy—I mean, this prick. My captor. "Well, I'm sorry you had to go through that."

After a pause, he asked, "Why do you care?" I think he looked over at me. I couldn't be sure since my hair was hanging in my face.

"Well… I don't know. Maybe I shouldn't but I've always had people who cared about me and I can't imagine what it would be like if they weren't in my life. God almighty, my mother must be clutching at her chest, telling everyone she's dying by now."

"Your mother has a heart condition?"

"Not a real one." I sighed. I thought about all the people who must be going out of their minds because of my disappearance, including the brothers I never had—my fellow cops. As much as I complained about their teasing, I secretly liked it. I knew they'd be concerned and looking for me, even though twenty-four hours hadn't passed yet. And poor Roger. He thinks I left him at the altar! How awful he must feel. I began to sniffle.

"Hey, don't start crying. You've been pretty brave so far. Don't make me regret letting you live."

"Well, forgive me for caring about people. I especially care about the innocent victims who sometimes get hurt, having done absolutely nothing to deserve it." I had hoped he'd make the connection. Either it went right over his head or he was ignoring my plight.

"So is that why you became a cop?"

"Yeah. That and other reasons."

"Like what?"

After a long pause, I realized I should have kept my mouth shut. "Forget it." Damn. Now I was the one who felt guilty. I fought my parents tooth and nail when it came to their plans for my life. They wanted me to go to college to find a nice Jewish man who would take care of me. A doctor, lawyer or businessman, like my father. When I did go to college, I majored in criminal justice. The only way they could deal with that is if I at least married a captain, or better yet, a city commissioner. I promised I wouldn't settle for anything less. Thus, I was still single at the age of thirty-eight.

"I doubt you're going to allow it but could I at least call my parents from a pay phone to let them know I'm alive?"

"You know I can't do that," he said in a low voice. "It's better if they think you've run away. I can't risk you telling them the truth." At my mournful look, he added, "Look, it's not like you gave me much choice."

Despite my wishing I could get a message to them, it would never erase what had happened. My parents would have already suffered the pain and humiliation of their daughter playing *the runaway bride*. Suddenly, I was so mad at myself, I couldn't focus any anger on Dorian.

Maybe I wouldn't have to. As soon as he was in jail, I'd never see him again. For some stupid reason that made me a little sad. *Get a hold of yourself, Faith. You know how charming sociopaths can be. Don't fall for his "It's not my fault" crap.*

"So are we getting close?"

"I don't know. Are we?"

"Huh? How should I know? You're the one at the damn wheel."

He chuckled. "Oh, is that what you meant? I thought maybe you were trying to have a personal conversation with me so we'd get to know each other, then I'd feel sorry for you and let you go."

"Of all the stupid ideas!" Okay, so we'd thought along the same lines. That only means he's smart, right?

We drove for another few minutes before he broke the silence. "To answer your question, we're almost there."

"I thought you were going to let me up as soon as we got off the highway."

"I changed my mind."

"Why?"

"You were being mouthy."

"Mouthy? That's what you call being mouthy? Boy, do you have a lot to learn about real women."

"Oh? And what sort of women do you think I know?"

He was trying to bait me again. I wasn't going to fall for it. If he got me flustered, I could miss an opportunity to escape. I had to stay as focused and dispassionate as possible. "Never mind. It really doesn't matter."

He swung the car hard to the left and my body leaned against the door. I wasn't going to complain, though. It might be considered "mouthy" and God forbid he would have to deal with that, again. He clearly didn't know what it was like for someone else to have an opinion of their own.

Then I heard the street noise fade into the background. The car descended a small hill and stopped.

    "Are we there, yet?"

Chapter Five and a Half
Dorian's side of the car

I was seriously hoping she was all talked out by the time we hit the road but no such luck. The second we started rolling, she started in with the questions again.

There she was, doubled over so she couldn't get oriented and she's asking, "So how did you get into BDSM, anyway?"

There was no beating around the bush with her, no pun intended. I considered not answering but it had been so long since anyone had questioned me beyond which whip or toys I preferred. Guess that was the downside of owning a business that tied into people's private lives. I owned the where, not the why. The why was reserved for shrinks, though there were a fair number of those in my membership too. It worked out well for referrals.

I'd never been to a shrink myself but it turned out that answering Faith felt good, so I did something I hadn't ever done before—I talked about my family. It kind of freaked me out how easy it felt, so I turned the tables on her to make it stop. Only she started to cry and I had to climb my way out of that one too.

The woman was trouble. Huh. Maybe that in itself was the allure. Yeah, that actually made sense. People tend to want most what they can't have and I only had her until she was hypnotized. I mean, I hate introspection as much as the next guy but I had to wonder what made her so special. Just because I planned to wipe it all from her memory didn't explain why I'd felt the need to talk about my family. I never had before, not even when it had felt like the grief was going to eat me alive.

I learned early on that mentioning I knew my parents were in the lifestyle was a mistake. No matter how I tried to explain that no, I didn't watch them "play" – *ew!* – and that it was no different than any kid figuring their parents had sex, people believed what they wanted to believe. I didn't even know the club existed until they'd died.

Yet I'd told Faith about them with little to no hesitation. Weird. I realized I needed to back off where she was concerned, which would have been easier if she didn't have the most incredible pussy I'd ever sunk my cock into. Oh, man. Even now, I wanted nothing more than to go balls deep again, as slowly as possible, feeling that silky inferno clasp me an inch at a time.

She already had enough info to bring down my little BDSM empire and the resources to make it happen. She was a cop, for Christ's sake! Yet all I could think about was getting between her legs again. Not even to pinch, spank or control her but to lose myself in that sweet pussy. Vanilla sex didn't feel so vanilla with her. It felt...voluntary. And so fucking hot that just the thought of getting back inside her was apparently frying my brain.

I nearly missed the turn into the office park and had to take a hard left. It pressed her up against the passenger door but it also shut off the endless questioning. For all of about two minutes.

Chapter Six
Faith in Dorian's world

You know how your body cramps up and gets stiff after a long ride with your head between your knees? No, maybe you don't. Well, trust me, it does. When I pivoted out of the car and Dorian unlocked the shackles and one handcuff, I leaned backward to get the kinks out. Looking up, I didn't see the warehouse as I'd expected but a different place altogether—a parking garage. "Where are we?"

"My office."

"I thought your office would be at the club."

He placed his wrist in the open cuff and clicked it shut. *Terrific. Now we're stuck with each other.*

"What club?"

Disgusted, I jammed my free hand on my hip. "Don't give me that innocent shit. Or do you own more than one?"

He chuckled and shook his head, then pulled me along behind him, saying, "No. I separate business from pleasure."

Ick.

"Let's go."

I wasn't about to walk three steps behind like a good little submissive so I quickly caught up and matched his stride.

Tucking his hands in his pockets brought my fingers close enough to his cock that I could probably have reached out and touched it—depending on how erect he was and whether or not it listed toward the left. Dammit. My mouth watered just picturing his silky, hard cock in my hand.

The elevator arrived, empty of passengers and we rode to the thirteenth floor. When the doors opened, I heard keyboards clacking behind closed doors. We strolled down the hall past some insurance office to a door marked Ds Enterprises. "How subtle."

"I like it," he said. He unlocked the door and ushered me inside. "Juliet should have dropped off some new clothes for you by now." He pointed to a large shopping bag on the black leather couch and said, "Ah. There they are."

As soon as he'd double and triple locked the door behind us, he unlocked my wrist cuff and I can't tell you how good it felt. I rubbed the soreness out, even before diving into the bag to see what Santa had brought. Okay, so I'm Jewish and shouldn't refer to Santa. But let me tell you, if the old man accidentally mixed up the addresses and mistook me for some girl on his nice list, I wouldn't have minded or given back the presents.

The first thing I pulled out of the bag floored me. A powder-blue vinyl dress—with the boobs cut out! I twisted it around to see the back and saw two matching low holes for the derriere. "Are you kidding me?"

Dorian had been headed for his massive safe but whirled around to see what my indignant cry was about. I held up the micro-mini Swiss cheese dress.

"What the hell?" His mouth hung open as he rushed to the couch and dumped the bag upside down. Out poured the most inappropriate pile of crap I'd ever seen. One black stretch jumpsuit sported a few strategically placed gold zippers, the most prominent of which came with a heart-shaped padlock at the top of the crotch. Must have been a chastity bodysuit. Another micro-mini dress had been fashioned of some material with as much coverage as a dyed spider web. Then, to add injury to insult, a pair of bright red spike heels so high they'd stand me up on my tiptoes.

Santa must have mixed me up with a girl on his naughty list. "Hmmm, these leave little to the imagination," I said. "Either, A, Juliet thinks I have such a great body I ought to show it off or B, she hates me. I'm pretty sure the answer is B."

Dorian still gaped as if he couldn't believe anyone might be passive-aggressive enough to deliberately misunderstand his orders. "How the hell am I supposed to get you on a plane in one of these?"

I shrugged. Anything I had to say would have been redundant.

* * * * *

Dorian double locked his office door and down the hall we strolled, wrist to wrist. He had printed out the photos Guy had taken—the ones of us kissing and tucked them into his inner jacket pocket, then made some extras to put into the safe. While he was in there, I heard something rustle as if he'd extracted something from another pocket. Lord knows what that could be. I didn't even have an engagement ring for him to steal. My mother insisted that I leave it in her hands so Roger could place the wedding ring on my bare finger, then later the diamond solitaire would sit above it. Tradition or something.

"Now where are you taking me?"

"I know of a small boutique owned by a friend of mine where we can find you some suitable clothes."

"A friend who wouldn't think twice about your being handcuffed to her customer?"

He flashed a genuine smile. "Now you're getting it."

Oh goody. Just what I always wanted—to understand the habits of a genuine BDSM aficionado. "Aren't you going to call Juliet and rip her a new one?"

"No."

"Why not? Don't you think her passive-aggressive behavior should be confronted?"

I could hear the elevator already on its way up, so I wondered how he was going to explain the handcuffs to whomever exited if it stopped on our floor.

"She obviously had her reasons and I don't have the time nor patience to listen to them. Don't worry. Suzanne has class. She carries only haute couture in her store."

"Unlike a certain Dominatrix I know of."

He tucked his hand behind his back, Napoleon-style and my arm followed, like it or not. Now he looked like some kind of arrogant general with a chick who couldn't keep her hands off him. Sheesh, what an ego.

Fortunately for him, there was no one getting off

the elevator as we got on. He looked down at me and winked—like we were co-conspirators or something. By the time we made it to the car, I had decided it might be best to let him think we were.

"Dorian, can you leave me unshackled? I promise I won't run."

"Why should I believe you?"

"Well, for one thing, we're going shopping. I've never welched on a shopping trip—ever."

He chuckled. "You're cute when you're not annoying the hell out of me."

At last. He might be letting his guard down. I relaxed my shoulders and warmth flowed into them, making me realize how tight I'd been holding my muscles. He opened my door and unchained himself from my wrist, meanwhile blocking any exit to freedom with his big, hunky body. If I wanted him to believe me, I had to play along for a while.

I settled into the butter-soft, leather seats and sank against the contoured back. "Ahhh... Much better than riding around like Quasimodo."

Without emotion, he said, "Fasten only your lap belt."

Why only the lap belt, I wondered. Was he going to make me lean over and shackle my wrist to my ankle, anyway? With a sigh, I did as he asked. Well, he didn't exactly ask but I did as he ordered, anyway.

He closed my door, jogged around to the other side and got in.

"See? I didn't try to escape."

"Smart move. This machine goes a couple hundred miles an hour, so I doubt you'd outrun me. Doing something like that would only anger me and then I'd have to cancel our shopping trip and make you wear the black jumpsuit."

"You don't think that would cause a stir at the airport? All those zippers would probably set off the metal detector."

"We could always drive."

I gasped. Was he serious? His mouth was set in a thin line so he looked deadly serious. "But... That would take—"

"I know. Days. And you'd be wearing that bodysuit the whole time. Unless..." He raised his eyebrows, wickedly, "you decided to change into the other outfits."

"Fat chance!" I almost gagged just thinking about it.

Finally, pouting on the inside, I said, "I'll be good." I even meant it, sort of. Unless presented with a guaranteed escape route, I'd bide my time until we were on the plane and in the air. I could probably enlist the help of the US Marshall on board at that time. I'm sure Dorian wouldn't try anything stupid against an *armed* law enforcement officer.

As long as I could get away before my mind was wiped, I could do my duty, clear my name and return to my life. Why, oh why, hadn't I strapped my service weapon to my leg under the wedding dress? It's not like there wasn't plenty of room under there.

"Lean over and face the floor so you can't see out the windows."

"Fine," I muttered and did as he willed.

* * * * *

As it turned out, I only had to keep my head down for about twenty minutes. I heard jackhammers and horns blowing. Something told me we hadn't returned to Waterloo, New Jersey. I mentioned that I had a slight touch of motion sickness. I didn't but I desperately wanted to identify the city. I suspected from the noise level, it might be the big apple. New York.

As soon as he said I could sit up, I recognized Newark. Oh well. I was sure they had a few nice stores too. Dorian was probably concerned about how a slumped-over body would look, even more than my ruining his lovely floor mat if I upchucked.

A few more turns and he pulled up alongside the curb in a newly renovated part of the city. Not too close to the airport, so I really didn't know the area at all. And I only occasionally visited the airport when I couldn't get a flight out of JFK.

He opened my door for me and reached for my hand to help me out. Then he slapped the cuff on me and to any passersby, we would appear as a well-dressed gentleman and a crazy lady. Maybe when I had some decent clothes we could skip the cuffs and resemble a normal, well-dressed couple. How odd it was to want that but I dismissed the thought, quickly.

Thankfully, we were only steps away from Suzanne's boutique—creatively named, *Suzanne's Boutique*. A pleasant atmosphere greeted us as we entered. A petite woman, presumably Suzanne, hurried over to us and air-kissed Dorian on both cheeks.

"Let me just lock the door and you can have the privacy you need," she said.

The woman seemed a bit hyperactive, or maybe she was just eager to please. I had a hard time picturing her as a Dom and suddenly the awful realization hit. Perhaps she was a sub—and one of Dorian's lovers. A stab of uncharacteristic hatred sliced through me as Dorian unlocked our wrists.

"We're looking for some traveling clothes."

"Would you like me to make some suggestions?

"Yes. Thank you, Suzanne." Dorian answered for me.

Get a grip, I told myself. So what if she was someone from his past? The place was stocked with all kinds of beautiful, color-coordinated, chic clothing and Dorian was footing the bill. Besides, we'd only shared one night of semi-kinky sex. It's not as if either of us wanted more, I lied to myself.

"You are a size eight, I think," she said.

"I don't know. Probably." I tried to remain casual but saying I looked a size smaller than my size ten uniform eased the sting considerably.

"I have some lovely business suits." She looked at Dorian. "Is that what you wanted?"

"Yes and I prefer pencil skirts," he said.

Naturally. Something I couldn't run in.

"Of course. I think you'd look marvelous in this coral ensemble. It's just right for your skin tone and—"

All I heard was blah, blah, blah as I gravitated toward a beautiful ivory pantsuit that she had displayed with a shimmering blue tank top and a printed silk scarf. Fingering the soft, lightweight fabric didn't make me want it less.

I had to have it. "Suzanne?"

"Yes, dahling?"

Oh. So now, I was *dahling*. She must not realize the nature of Dorian's and my relationship. Maybe I could use that?

"I love this pantsuit but I can't identify the material. What is it made of?"

"That's washable silk. Very travel-worthy, not only because it can be hand washed but it doesn't wrinkle easily. And good news! I have the pencil skirt in the same color and fabric."

Oh, goody gumdrops. The bondage skirt.

"Could I interest you in a coral camisole and scarf to go with it? You'd look fabulous in this with the latest season's colors."

I wasn't crazy about coral to begin with and it was just different enough to act as a neon sign if I did get away. "I really like the blue. May I try it just the way you've put it together here?"

Again, she looked to Dorian. He nodded, thank goodness, so I was off to the dressing room with it.

By the time I had the whole outfit on and had checked all the angles—butt not too big, hips not too tight, boobs not flattened—I stepped out of the dressing room to Dorian, who was holding two glasses of wine.

"I thought you might like some refreshment."

"Yes, please." I swiped the glass within close reach and poured a generous gulp down my throat. "Man, that really hits the spot. I needed that."

He smiled. "Drink up and I'll get you another."

"No, thanks. One is fine." I had to stay sharp as much as I'd have loved to get blotto and forget this whole mess.

"Turn around," he said, eyeing the outfit.

I did a slow twirl.

"Very nice. But you need some heels to go with it."

"Oh, I don't wear high-heels very well. How about flats or a pair of kitten heels?"

"You seemed quite comfortable in your white satin

shoes."

"It must have been the adrenaline."

"I took the liberty of picking some out for you."

That's when I noticed the tall, black leather pumps. My plan to get some running shoes wasn't panning out the way I would have liked.

"Try them on."

My feet slipped into them as easily as Cinderella's foot matched the glass slipper. Why couldn't I have slippers? Those would be nice. "I don't think they go with the rest of the outfit."

He scowled. "Wear them around the store while you select something else that will go with the shoes, then."

"You must really like these shoes."

"Suzanne said they would go with everything."

"Except what I'm wearing." I folded my arms, proving I could be as stubborn as he was.

"Fine. Stay here then, I'll have Suzanne find something else for you to try on."

I reached out and grabbed his arm. "No way. She'll put me in head to toe coral."

"Fine, I'll tell her no coral."

"I'll tell her." I pushed past him and stomped into the showroom, hoping he didn't follow and cuff me for being mouthy, again. On my way past a dress rack, I glanced at the section holding my size and noticed a couple items in solid black. That might please both of us. It would go with the shoes he liked and help me disappear into the shadows should I slip away in the night.

I pulled one of them off the rack. It seemed to float on the air. It was a simple sleeveless shift but shaped like a woman. Very Audrey Hepburn-ish.

I turned around to see Dorian slowly coming toward me, sipping his wine.

"I like this one," I said.

He nodded. "Try it on. I'll get you another glass of wine."

"But I just said—"

He whirled on his flat leather heel and walked off toward the back room.

Whatever... I fumed as I marched back to the dressing room. By the time I had zipped the gorgeous black chiffon dress, Suzanne appeared with a different pair of shoes.

"Oh, that's lovely on you! I found some shoes for the other outfit but I hope you'll get this one. You look stunning in it."

I was beginning to hate her less and less with each compliment. Now she held a pair of dove gray shoes with an open toe and moderate heel.

"Can I try those shoes? They look comfortable and super cute."

Dorian entered behind her and stopped dead in his tracks. He eyed me up and down as if he'd never met me—but wanted to.

"We'll take that."

I couldn't help smiling. He didn't even ask how much it cost. He just bought it on sight. Bam, like that. I'd never bought anything in my life without checking the price tag first. I usually checked even before trying things on in case, God forbid, I ripped the seam or something.

"Wonderful!" Suzanne squealed and applauded.

Hmmm... It must have cost plenty.

Dorian handed me the glass of wine. "We'll take the other outfit too." He held up his glass in a toast, so we clinked glasses and drank. "Now we need a little lingerie."

Suzanne rushed off with visions of dollar signs dancing in her head.

"Do the shoes I sent in fit?" He nodded at the new gray ones.

"You picked these out?"

"You seem surprised."

"Well, yeah." I took another gulp of champagne. "I mean, these are stylish and comfortable. Not like the come-fuck-me pumps I expected you to insist I wear."

"Are you calling the black ones, 'Come fuck me' pumps?"

"Well, kind of. The heels are a little high and spiky but I can wear them. They look too damn good with this dress to just dismiss them out of hand."

"Good. I'm glad we agree. Finish your wine. We're almost done here."

I noticed my head clouding over as if I'd drunk a magnum instead of two glasses. "I think I've had enough." Feeling more than woozy, I swayed and the last thing I remember was falling into his strong arms.

Chapter Six and a Half
Never trust a Dominatrix to pick out clothes

Every single article of clothing Juliet had left for Faith was completely unsuitable for a plane ride, even one to Las Vegas. Hell, they would have been questionable for the Isle of Hedonism. Juliet was a dead woman. At the very least she wasn't going to get a cake and I was going to make sure she didn't steal it from Guy, either.

This meant more delays but there was nothing I could do about it. We had to go see Suzanne in Newark. At least it wasn't too far out of our way to the airport and there was no doubt Suzanne would be discreet. Last time I'd seen her had been about a month ago at the club when she'd been presenting her perfect ass for paddling with a wooden hairbrush, so we both had a lot to be discreet about. Her for wanting it done and me for doing the deed.

Not that Faith would have appreciated either side of that story. Man, I had to get her out of there fast before she bombarded Suzanne with questions and wore her down too. Besides, we had a plane to catch. Except that's when Bridezilla turned into Shopzilla and she wouldn't be hurried along. Christ, who the fuck cared what color the blouse was or if the shoes went with every zipper and button on the outfit? Wasn't it all better than a minidress with the tits cut out?

When she finally made her choices, she turned to me and I was floored by how much I wanted her. If we'd had time, I would have ordered Suzanne to leave so I could take Faith right up against the dressing room mirror. We didn't have time but I did take a few minutes to send Suzanne off for some lingerie and to give Faith a second glass of wine. The former because who knew how much time it would take to get her hypnotized and I believed in being prepared. The latter because I needed to slip her another mickey. The first potion in her champagne only made her mellow. She needed another for the plane ride.

Chapter Seven
Las Vegas, here we come

I came to, sort of, in a first class seat on the way to Vegas. Dorian had his arm around me, conveniently propping me up and I vaguely recollected being rolled through the airport in a wheelchair.

"Whash happening? Where da hell am I?" And what had happened to my power of speech? I seemed to be slurring my words.

"There, there, darling. You just had a little too much to drink. You'll feel better soon."

"Too much? I had two glasshes of champagne!"

"But on an empty stomach. I should have insisted you eat lunch but you said you didn't want any."

"Really?" Since when did I refuse a free lunch? Oh, speaking of free, I glanced down and saw the black dress and pumps I had been wearing when I was last conscious. "Oh, thank you for da nice dressh. Hey look! There's a bag from Shushanne's under the next sheat. Did the couple in front of us go there too?"

Dorian grinned. "No, those are yours, darling."

"Huh? Tha's right. I 'member now. You said you were buying the shuit too."

"Yes, I bought the suit you liked so much and some pretty lingerie."

"Lemme see." I leaned over, grabbed the bag but couldn't right myself until Dorian grabbed my shoulder and hauled me back into the cushy seat.

"Whew. I guess zat champagne was pretty shtrong." I pawed through the bag to find not only the gray shoes and ivory suit, covered in plastic but also the blue top nicely folded in tissue paper and two silk scarves. Hmm… Why two, I wondered.

"Where's da… Oh, here it is!" I yanked a white, lace bra out of a separate smaller bag and it whapped the back of my seat. "Oops." I giggled. And giggled—and giggled some more. In fact, I couldn't stop giggling.

The flight attendant strolled over. "Ah, you're awake. I understand congratulations are in order."

"For waking up?"

She just smiled and I giggled. "I gots da giggles," I said and she grinned.

"Would you like something to drink?"

"Oh, no, no, no." I shook my head vigorously and then couldn't make it stop. "No more for me."

"Coffee, then?" she offered.

I could see she wasn't going to be happy until I let her get me something. Why did she suddenly remind me of my mother?"

"Kay. Coffeesh good."

As soon as she left, I cozied up to Dorian, who looked particularly handsome and virile at the moment. "What a nice man. You are sho good to me,

Roger."

Oops. I had just called him by the wrong name. Either he didn't catch it or didn't care, because all he said was, "You're more than welcome, my love."

What was all this lovey-dovey talk about? Had we gotten married or something when I was out of it? Suddenly the awful possibility vibrated through me like a shock wave. I gasped. "We didn't get married when I washn't looking, did we?"

He turned to face me, squarely and propped his forehead against mine. "Would you like that?"

I launched into a fresh case of the giggles. At last, the flight attendant returned. Ahhh...saved by the coffee. But did I use the distraction to drop the subject? No. Of course not. With all my defenses down, I blathered on.

"I really like you. You are genrus, nice to look at and you make love like a...a...funny bunny."

Now the whole first class section was giggling. There was that three-second delay as what I had said registered and then I burst out laughing.

Dorian, however, didn't appear to be amused.

Chapter Seven and One Quarter
Dorian interjects— For men everywhere

I got precisely two hours of silence before Faith woke up, then six minutes and twenty-two seconds before she managed to embarrass me and herself by flinging a bra around and calling her new "husband" by the wrong name. Okay, so no one else in first class knew my name wasn't Roger but they did think it was I who made love like a "funny bunny." Whatever the hell that meant.

I had a more important question. Who the fuck was Roger? The real fiancé she'd left at the altar? I'd made love to this woman, damn it. The last thing I wanted to hear was some other guy's name coming from those lush lips. Vanilla style, my ass. Or more aptly, hers. For the first time, I wished we were in my club so I could punish her properly, then show her what else she could do with that mouth.

It was to her benefit that she fell asleep on the plane a couple more times and she groggy enough to be subdued until we got to the hotel room in Vegas. By that time I'd calmed down a bit, though, I still wanted to paint her ass red with my palm. That wasn't going to happen by consent—not at that point, anyway. The blowjob was another matter entirely.

Chapter Seven and a Half
Who's on top?

"A funny bunny, huh?" Dorian crawled over our Vegas hotel room bed like a panther and pounced on me, grinning.

I laughed, still feeling a bit tipsy. Like most people, after some time had passed, he was able to see the humor in the situation and join in the fun.

He growled in my ear. "How many bunnies do you know who can do to you what I can do?" Then he sucked on my earlobe.

"Oh!" I squealed and giggled. "None. Nada. Not one."

Emboldened by my lack of restraint and the craving in my already-damp panties, I launched myself at him and managed to flip him onto his back and pin him there. His grin turned to surprise and then slowly returned.

With my defenses lowered, I found myself saying all sorts of strange things. "Maybe I'm the funny bunny because all I want to do is fuck."

"And it looks like you want to be the top."

"Yup. The top dog. Well, not a dog exactly. I don't want you to think of me as a dog," I babbled.

"Don't worry, I don't." He clasped the back of my head and drew me to his lips, delivering a deep, drawn out kiss that left me breathless. Then he rolled over and I was underneath him again. "You can think of me as the top dog, though. Wouldn't bother me a bit."

Why did his expression remind me of Wolfie? And why was I suddenly more concerned about my dress than about Dorian? Maybe Juliet was right and I was a J.A.P. after all. With all of this back and forth motion, my dress had bunched up around my waist and thighs and I couldn't stand the thought of crumpling it.

"Damn. My beautiful dress must be getting wrinkled."

"We're wearing entirely too many clothes anyway. Let me help you take yours off." He flipped me onto my stomach as if I were a hotdog on the grill.

I heard the rasp of a zipper and felt cool air on my back.

His husky voice said, "Pull your upper body out of the dress."

How did he figure I was going to do that? I quit yoga after one class. Still, I wanted the dress off as much as he did, so I slithered out of it using whatever the heck that position was called. Downward facing spineless dog? Dragon doing push-ups? Sorry. I had been paying more attention to the pain than the names of the supposedly relaxing stretches.

"Okay, I'm out. Now get off me so I can—"

Without waiting for me to finish my sentence, Dorian lifted himself onto his knees beside me and yanked my dress down and off, flinging it across the room.

"Hey!"

"Sorry, dear. I get impatient when I'm teased."

"Who's teasing?" I wanted him badly and that bothered me—a little. It didn't bother me enough to stop me, though. I knew I was in trouble when "Stockholm, here I come," popped out of my mouth.

He stripped quickly and I carefully removed my new lingerie. "Ohhh, pretty! Lavender lace." Didn't know what happened to my old white panties, corset and stockings but I also didn't care. Now *that* was weird!

Dorian's hard cock seemed even larger than before. Impossible. Maybe he used one of those pump things? Nah, I couldn't see him doing that. Then I came up with the crazy idea that he might be more aroused than usual. Aroused by me. *Me?*

"I just want to ram my rod into your tight cunt and fuck you like crazy."

"Very romantic."

He looked at me funny and I had to remind myself that falling for him was a very bad idea. It must be hard to arrest someone you love.

"But if that's what you really want to do…" I shrugged.

His eyes narrowed and he frowned. "No. I think you need more than that." Without warning, he bounded off the bed and reached into the bag with my new clothes. I couldn't see what he had in his hand but I had a bad feeling about it. Suddenly he flashed one of the scarves he'd bought me. I sat up so he couldn't get my wrists near the headboard. Instead, he grabbed my foot and lickety-split, he tied my foot to the footboard!

"Wait, remember Stockholm? I don't need that."

"Personally, I think you need to be spanked until your backside is hot and numb but that would probably just turn you off."

Shock waves rippled through me—followed by something else. Excitement? Titillation? Oh God. What was happening to me?

He lay beside me and pulled me into his arms. His expression softened. "If you could trust me and I could trust you, you wouldn't need that smart mouth of yours and you wouldn't make me want to discipline you. In fact, I could see me showering you with affection. Taking care of you. Protecting you." A tender kiss followed his unexpected, caring words.

I didn't know what to say. For once in my life, I had no smart-ass comeback. All I wanted to do was curl up in his warmth and bask in it—if my foot was free, of course. When he pulled away from my lips, I slipped my hand behind his head and brought him back for another one—and another and another.

"I have an idea," he said. After another trip to the clothing bag, he returned with the other scarf.

"Oh, no. I'm not into the bondage thing and besides, I'm ready and willing, like I said."

"This isn't for your wrists or ankles," he said, seductively. "This is your blindfold."

He came toward me as he folded it corner to corner.

"Wait just a minute. Don't you want me to see what I'm doing? I mean, what if I grab the wrong thing or bend it the wrong way?"

He just laughed and rolled the scarf on the oblique. "I want you to know how it feels to trust someone."

"I can trust. I trust people who are trustworthy."

"I doubt you have ever trusted completely…or intimately. Go with it. I think you'll be surprised how good it feels. Plus, if you take away one of the senses all of the others are heightened. I'm not talking about bondage where one person makes all the decisions and takes all the responsibility with only your happiness in mind—this time."

Thoughts whirled through my head. I'd still have my hands free and could rip off the blindfold at any time. And I could still untie my foot if the last scarf was around my head and not my opposite wrist. "Okay, I'll take the risk."

"Good. I know you'll like it."

I lifted my head while he wrapped the blindfold around my eyes and tied it in back but slightly to the side, tightly. Then he placed a pillow beneath my neck.

"Comfortable?"

"Uh-huh."

I felt the mattress dip on one side of the bed and sensed his body heat and something else. It was as though I could feel his magnetic essence closing in. His hand traveled over my whole body, seductively, caressing me, finding new sensitive places I didn't know I had.

I shivered when he touched my ribs and he lowered his head to kiss each one, traveling down my left side and up my right. I arched when he found my breast and scraped his tongue over my nipple. After laving it for a good long time, he latched onto my aching areola and sucked. Ripples of pleasure coursed through me from my nipples to my clenching womb.

I don't think my womb had ever clenched before.

"Dorian," I whispered.

He didn't stop to respond, thank goodness. I had nothing to say other than his name. Eventually, he sucked my other breast just as thoroughly and I undulated with lust.

I wanted more of him. All of him. "Please, I need you," I begged.

"Already?" I heard the smile in his voice.

"Yes. Now." Hot and bothered barely described how badly I burned for him.

He reached into the bedside table's drawer where he'd put his condoms, yet he said, "Don't I get any foreplay?"

"Fore— You need foreplay?" Guys needed foreplay? I'd never heard of that. I thought they were pretty much ready to march as soon as the flag was raised. Yet, it seemed only fair to return the favor.

"Um…okay. What do you want?"

He rolled over onto his back took my hand and stroked his cock with it. "What do you think I want?"

Oral? Uh-oh. I thought that maybe if I played dumb I could get away without having to go down on that monster.

"Oh, sure. I can do that." I surrounded his cock with my hand—well, almost—and took over stroking him with the same motion he had been using.

Chuckling, he said, "Can't bring yourself to give me a blowjob, huh? Didn't think so."

I knew I had just been insulted. "What? You don't think I would? What makes you say that?"

He didn't respond but I could picture his infuriating, knowing grin.

"Hey, I could if I wanted to."

He said, "Sure you could…" as if daring me to. Suddenly an old joke popped into my head. *What's the only thing a Jewish-American Princess will go down on? Answer—The escalator at Bloomingdales.* Har, har. Damned if I'd let him think I wouldn't or couldn't.

"Okay, suddenly I want to." I grabbed the base of his cock, rolled up on my elbow, scooted down, bobbed around until I found it and inserted as much as I could into my mouth. It was like trying to eat a salami, whole. Well too bad. I'd prove I— *Hey!* Suddenly, I knew what he was doing. He knew that if he said I wouldn't, I would. *Damn him.* I fell right into his trap. I never said I was the brightest candle in the Menorah.

I stroked him with my mouth a few times, then pulled back and pleaded with my sexiest voice. "Honestly, Dorian. I'm so hot for you, I can't wait."

He chuckled. "I just wanted to see if you'd really do it. Stay where you are, honey. I'm gonna take you from behind, doggy style."

Like I had a choice. Truth be told, even if I did, I'd choose to fill my drenched center with his cock, immediately.

He stood, I heard the rip of the foil packet and waited a moment while he applied his condom and then he untied my foot. That was a surprise. "Get on your knees. It's time I showed you how to respect the top dog."

Rolling my eyes under the blindfold, I did as he asked. If he tried something disgusting, at least I was in a good position to run, or crawl, away.

He positioned himself behind me and thrust his cock into my slick vagina, *thank God,* and I sighed my relief.

"Feels good, doesn't it? I can get deeper in this position and give you a nice reach-around at the same time."

Leaning against my back, he cupped my mons with his hand and fucked me slowly at the same time as he caressed my pussy.

"You want me to touch your clit, don't you?"

"God, yes!"

"Will you be a good girl from now on? Realize I've been more than kind to you and treat me accordingly?"

I was dying for his touch. "Yes, oh yes!"

He pulled his cock back to my entrance and stopped. "Promise?"

Gritting my teeth, I ground out, "I promise. I don't have to call you sir, though, do I?"

"Not unless you want to." Resuming his motion, he said, "I'll reward you for your promise now but don't disappoint me later. I won't tolerate disrespect."

With that, he placed his talented finger on my clit and rubbed as he plundered my channel. I moaned in ecstasy. Really. I'd never been with anyone like this. Of course, he owned a sex club, so he'd probably had plenty of practice. A stab of jealousy twisted my gut as I pictured him in the middle of threesomes and orgies.

I began to pound against him. He matched my frantic rhythm and soon we both panted with the effort. How he managed to stay right on my clit during all the frenetic activity I didn't know but I loved it. Maybe he was right about needing a skilled lover, because the sensations of a building climax seemed stronger. Familiar spasms began to rack my body as my moans threatened to turn to screams. I buried my face in the pillow and let go. As I climaxed, I shook violently and, I swear my spirit soared right out of my body.

Dorian jerked hard several times as he found his release. His grunts sounded as if he was pushing an anvil uphill. When he had experienced his last aftershock, we collapsed together and lay there, gasping for breath.

At some point, during the afterglow, I realized that I couldn't have been drunk on two glasses of champagne. It just wasn't possible to be that out of it even for a lightweight like me. I had to have been drugged. And I knew just the controlling jerk who would do something like that.

I ripped off the blindfold. "Dorian?"

"Yes?"

I propped myself against the headboard and crossed my arms. "You suck. You drugged me."

He sat up and raised his eyebrows.

"Don't even think about denying it."

"I wasn't going to."

"Because if you think for one minute I might believe... Wait a minute. Did you say you weren't going to deny it?"

"I know you well enough to know you wouldn't buy a crock of shit like that. Most cops have a good idea when they're being outright lied to. Besides, I'm not a very good liar."

"Ha! Yeah, right. Then how did you make the airline crew think I was drunk?"

"That was easy. I said you'd had a celebratory send-off with your girlfriends since they couldn't go with us to the wedding. People believe what they want to believe. They chose to let you on that plane thinking we might miss our own wedding."

Fuck. Now I understood why the flight attendant wanted to congratulate me and why Dorian had been calling me darling. Furthermore, he didn't look at all contrite. I wanted to punch him in the stomach—so I did.

"Ouch. What was that for?"

"Are you kidding? You drugged me and then lied to me about it."

"No, I didn't." He shrugged. "Well, I mean, yes, I drugged you, but I didn't lie about it. You just didn't ask."

Now I was pissed. "Ever hear of lying by omission?"

He shrugged. "I didn't trust you enough not to spill the beans and yell for help on the plane. I figured if you looked drunk people would just think you were raving or talking nonsense." He smiled. "You are a funny drunk, though."

I had to hit him again. I don't know why. I just did.

"Cut that out!"

"Oh, sure, but it's all right if *you* hit people, huh?"

"Only if they pay me to do it."

Exasperated, I felt like I was fighting a losing battle. There was no way he would ever see that what he did was strange. I had hoped that maybe I could sway him. He certainly seemed to enjoy our pain-free sexual liaisons.

"Look. I'm not asking a lot. I agreed to have my mind wiped, I agreed to go to Vegas with you, but I did not agree to be drugged."

"Your agreement didn't matter. I have to do what I have to do. I think we both know that the alternative isn't an option."

"Okay. I get it. You, Dorian. Me, hostage. But that's not the only option." Turning himself in was an option. A very viable option. But what could I say? *I think you ought to go to the police and confess right now?*

Dorian slipped out from under the king size sheets and stretched with his back to me. Holy schnitzels! Taut muscles rippled from his broad shoulders to his tapered waist and clenched again from his glutes to his thighs and calves. He shivered slightly with the effort.

"Fuck," I muttered.

He gazed over his shoulder at me. "Something wrong?" Then he turned and stood with his hands on his hips and his semi-automatic weapon dangling between his thighs.

I reached for the telephone he had unplugged. "Hello, Stockholm? Yeah, I have your syndrome and I'd like to return it."

He smiled. "I wish I could believe…" He shook his head and the smile vanished.

"What? That I have Stockholm Syndrome or that I want to get rid of it?"

"No…" he stopped and I waited. I thought he was about to say something nice to me. Maybe beginning with, "If only things were different" or something like that. But, no. He just shook his head again and said, "Let's take a shower."

My jaw dropped. "Together?"

He eyed me with a sensuous grin. "Of course. When in Sweden…"

Chapter Seven and Three Quarters
What's good for the gander

It took less than six minutes and twenty-two seconds after entering our room before she was tossing around her lingerie again. This time, I was fine with it. In fact, she was naked and I was ready to fuck her deep and hard without a single lick to Mr. Happy. Christ, watching her undulate her way out of her clothes had really set me on edge.

I thought she'd want to hear about it. "I just want to ram my rod into your tight cunt and fuck you like crazy."

"Very romantic. But if that's what you really want to do…" she shrugged.

Clearly it wasn't what she wanted me to do. Holy shit! Was the submissive in her making an appearance? The desire to spank her had been put on the back burner but hell, it wouldn't take much to rev it up again. A couple of sentences out of her mouth usually did the trick.

What the hell. Just to be on the safe side, I got one

of the scarves and tied her foot to the footboard. Then I gave it a shot. "Personally, I think you need to be spanked until your backside is hot and numb but that would probably just turn you off."

Bingo. She tried to hide it but I could see the spark of excitement at the idea of being turned over my knee. Oh yeah. It excited me too, in a way I hadn't felt in years of enacting harsh discipline. Kind of like going back to the excitement of that first kiss in my youth.

Once again, I used the opportunity to explain the gentle side of the BDSM lifestyle. In a way, I felt like I was just truly starting to understand it myself. Weird. I ran with it and hot damn if she wasn't game. She agreed to having her foot tied, agreed to a blindfold… I figured I stood a good chance of getting that blowjob too.

I didn't expect her to suck at it. At least not in a bad way. Seeing my dick in her hand being guided to her open mouth was great but she wasn't very enthusiastic about actually doing the deed. I made a mental note to string a designer label around the base of my cock next time. After her excitement over the purchases we'd made at Suzanne's, I was willing to bet she'd go deep for couture and probably swallow if I added a sale sticker.

But for that moment, those few strokes in her mouth were enough. More than enough. I had won. I felt like beating my chest and howling to the moon but at the same time I was trying not to laugh. I was having fun.

Jesus. Wouldn't that go over well at the club. Submissives didn't tend to care for Doms who gave stern orders and punishment with a goofy smile. But

Faith and I weren't at the club and I didn't need to play Dom. Not to the normal extent, anyway, just enough to get me what I wanted.

What I wanted was to show Faith how very good I could be. I grabbed a condom and untied her foot. "Get on your knees. It's time I showed you how to respect the top dog."

She did and the sight of her wet pussy peeking out from under her lush ass nearly undid me. I thrust deep, noting with satisfaction that she was more than ready for me. That was nice but I wanted her screaming.

Bracing myself, I reached around and slid my hand between her legs. *Damn!* She was so wet, so hot that I had to fight for control again. But I was determined to give her something concrete to understand about my lifestyle. About me.

"You want me to touch your clit, don't you?" I bent my index finger and ran it over her slick folds, touching her everywhere but where she wanted it most.

"God, yes!"

"Will you be a good girl from now on? Realize I've been more than kind to you and treat me accordingly?"

"Yes, oh yes!"

It was a start. I made her beg, then beg some more. I didn't expect to have to hold back my own cries as my body took over. I'd managed to keep my finger on her clit and rode her through her orgasm, then I grasped her hips and pulled her ass hard against me, shaking right along with her as I came.

Fuckin' A! It was all I could do to take care of the necessities and fall back on the bed to concentrate on breathing. Sex with her just got better and better.

I should have known I wouldn't get to revel long in the silent afterglow.

"Dorian?"

"Yes?"

"You suck. You drugged me."

Shit. I sat up and looked at her. She'd ripped off the blindfold and was propped against the headboard, arms crossed. There was definitely no avoiding the moment.

"Don't even think about denying it," she warned.

"I wasn't going to."

I was surprised when she slugged me in the stomach. She'd finally asked the right questions and I had answered them truthfully. We both knew I deserved to get hit lower.

It should have ended there, but I couldn't resist teasing her about being a funny drunk.

She hit me again, this time right above the danger zone. Close enough that I changed my mind about deserving it. "Cut that out!"

"Oh, sure but it's all right if *you* hit people, huh?"

"Only if they pay me to do it."

She shook her head at me, clearly disappointed. I still wasn't sure why but I wasn't about to prolong the conversation—or get hit again—by asking her to explain.

"Look," she tried again, "I'm not asking a lot. I agreed to have my mind wiped, I agreed to go to Vegas with you but I did not agree to be drugged."

She sounded like she was talking to a four year old. Not a smart tone to take with a Dom, even one who knew he deserved it. All that talk about trusting me and I'd drugged her when the shoe was on the other foot. I wished things could have been different and nearly told her so but her shoe was a stiletto and the wearer was a cop.

It wasn't her problem that it was getting harder and harder to remember that. Hell, it was getting hard to remember anything but how it felt to be with her. And in her.

"Your agreement didn't matter," I attempted to get the derailed control back on track. "I have to do what I have to do. I think we both know that the alternative isn't an option."

"Okay. I get it. You, Dorian. Me, hostage. But that's not the only option."

What, like turning myself in? Right. This conversation was over.

I slipped out from under the sheets and stretched with my back to her, testing my muscles to make sure they were rejuvenated. The ones in my thighs and ass trembled a bit but hey, they'd been used pretty hard.

"Fuck," Faith muttered.

I looked over my shoulder at her. She was staring at my ass. "Something wrong?"

She reached for the telephone I had unplugged earlier. "Hello, Stockholm? Yeah, I have your syndrome and I'd like to return it."

That made me smile. "I wish I could believe…"

I shook my head and just like that, I realized how sad it was that I couldn't explore having a real relationship with this woman.

"What? That I have Stockholm Syndrome or that I want to get rid of it?"

"No…" I stopped myself from admitting I would even want to try anything beyond sex. It wasn't going to happen. Sex, on the other hand, was another matter. "Let's take a shower."

Her jaw dropped. "Together?"

I gave her my best "let's fuck" grin. "Of course. When in Sweden…"

She went for it, which made it all the more difficult to leave her hot and bothered and tied to the shower bar but it had to be done. My friend Ivan had agreed to help me out and he was waiting in the hotel lounge.

Chapter Eight
I shoulda had a V8, even a V-6 would do

I realized why the idea of bondage had never appealed to me. It was for this very reason. There I stood, drip-drying in the shower with my wrists bound and trussed up like a turkey—while Dorian went "*out*". I had already tested the strength of the acrylic grab bar but it seemed to have been built right into the shower enclosure itself. Even allowing it to take my full, dead weight didn't budge it.

My only hope was for either Dorian to return or for these silk scarves to break. Fat chance. Silk could be deceptively strong and Dorian said he'd be gone for "a while", whatever that meant. A few hours? A couple of days? A week? His self-serving deviousness infuriated me and I no longer cared about how sexy he was, or how generous, or how his smooth, masculine voice turned me to putty. This was just unacceptable behavior. Our sexual relationship had definitely hit the skids. Or as they say, the fat lady had left the building. Well, something like that.

I heard wheels rolling down the carpeted hallway. What if housekeeping found me like this? No. I was sure Dorian had hung the *do not disturb* sign on the outside of the door. He thought of everything. That's one of those double-edged-sword traits. It's great if he's packing for you. Not so great if he decides to buy a couple of silk scarves knowing that handcuffs smuggled through airport security would send out red flags. Top dog, huh? He was *so* in the doghouse, if and when he got back. It was that "if" idea that had me verging on panic.

Maybe I wanted housekeeping to find me. Why not? The humiliation wouldn't last long. As soon as I got dressed, I'd escape and never see Las Vegas again.

Then it occurred to me that escaping might be the easy part. After that I was on my own with no money, two thousand miles from home. I could call the cops, *try* to explain what happened and hope they'd send me back to Waterloo, New Jersey—after taking my statement, verifying my identity, arresting Dorian and deposing me. Or I could call my father and ask him to wire money for a plane ticket, knowing my mother would demand to talk to me, then cry, yell and heap on the guilt. Well, as Scarlett O'Hara would say, "I'll worry about that tomorrow".

The wheels rolled closer and when I estimated the maid might be right outside our door, I shouted for help. Anticipating rescue, I stopped to hear if the lock was rattling. Nothing. The cart continued to roll by. I yelled for help again and this time I added, "I'm tied up." To my horror, I heard a woman laughing. Laughing! Apparently screams and bondage were an everyday occurrence here. *Damn Vegas.*

I fought against the scarves and noticed they

seemed to be lengthening. That's right! Fabric had a tendency to stretch when wet. It was worth a shot.

Balancing on one foot, I turned on the shower with the other one. Fortunately, some of the spray hit the scarves and I pulled—and pulled—and pulled! Eventually one of the loops lengthened enough to wrest my hand from it. I unwrapped the other one and noticed red marks around my wrists. Ha. That should convince the police that I was telling the truth. Yup, I had decided the cops were the preferred alternative to calling my family.

After drying and dressing, I was ready to make a run for it. I grabbed the bag of clothes, sans the nasty scarves and charged toward the stairs. The elevator was approaching the top floor and if it happened to be Dorian, he was less likely to find me on a lower floor. Bounding down the stairs, I rushed to the elevator and reached it before it left the top floor. Thank God for small favors. Jabbing at the down button repeatedly, I hoped it wouldn't pass by in favor of some earlier command. Fortunately, it stopped and the doors whooshed open. At last it seemed as if my luck had improved.

I pushed the button that said *LL* and leaned against the cold, metal wall, anxiously waiting to land at the lower lobby. Just in case it helped speed things up, I punched the *LL* button a couple more times.

It didn't. It stopped at almost every floor to pick up passengers on the way down. I wished I had boarded the express instead of the local. Most folks got off on the floor marked with a single *C* and I saw why when the doors opened. The casino echoed with an assortment of irritating noises that could drive me crazy in a heartbeat. Ding-ding-ding. Dong-dong-

dong.

I let the clothing bag drop to the floor in order to block my ears while waiting for the doors to whoosh closed again. The clanging finally stopped when I reached my floor. I bent over to pick up my bag and when I straightened up, I saw that *LL* must have stood for lower level. I was in the parking garage. So much the better. I could slip out onto the street without being seen other than by the two guys coming toward me.

When I recognized the swagger, I froze. Dorian took only a second to recognize me and react, then he called out to the other guy, "There she is!"

I dashed toward the sound of traffic with both of them racing after me. Could I run faster without the bag of clothes? Probably. Did I want to abandon the striking Audrey Hepburn dress and matching black heels? Nope. I could carry them a tiny bit longer.

When it was clear that Dorian was gaining on me, I made the hard but appropriate decision and tossed the bag into his path. He leapt over it and continued to close in. *Damn.* I couldn't see where the other guy was. Maybe he didn't care enough about Dorian's little problem to join the foot chase.

I heard an engine revving and the screech of tires. Soon a vehicle roared up behind me. I didn't dare take my eye off the prize. Daylight. Freedom. Please, God, just one more burst of speed… Dorian must have prayed for the same thing because he grabbed me around my waist and we both tumbled into the gutter by the side of the ramp.

His buddy screeched to a halt and jumped out of the car. "Why the hell did you rescue her? I thought she was trying to put you in jail."

"Calm down, Ivan. I don't want to complicate things with a murder charge." He dragged me, swearing, over to the car and opened the passenger's side door. "Get in, darling. We have a hypnotist to meet."

Ivan shook his head. "I thought you said she was tied up."

"She was." Dorian looked at me and if I wasn't mistaken, a little respect was mixed with the aggravation in his expression. "How did you get out of the room?"

"Ha, wouldn't you like to know?"

He glared. "The maid didn't go in there, did she?"

"Why, did you tell her not to?"

"I *paid* her not to."

"Here, use my cuffs." Ivan handed the shiny, metal bracelets to the fiend squeezing my guts.

"Thanks, Ivan."

I launched into a litany of swear words that would make a war veteran blush.

"I'm not taking any chances with you, sweetheart. Where you go, I go," and he snapped his left wrist to my right.

Now that I had my breath back, I decided to give him a piece of my mind—unless his accomplice had a ball gag.

"You son of a bitch. What's the matter with you? Does it give your puny self-esteem a boost to tie up women and leave them? Do you get a charge out of knowing they're helpless without you? That all they can do is wait for your return and let you push them around some more? What a friggin' awesome way to treat a lover."

He gave me a cold stare, then retorted. "My self-esteem is just fine and you know why I can't trust you not to run off."

Yeah, I did. And at the first opportunity I'd do so again so there wasn't much I could say in response to that.

"Why can't you understand my position, Faith? You want to arrest me for the way I make my living and my whole friggin' lifestyle. You're trying to ruin my life."

"Look, I do understand but I have a sworn obligation to uphold the law. You're breaking it, so you *should* go to jail."

Dorian rolled his eyes. "Think for a moment. Turn off your rigid cop doctrine and think as a person who believes in freedom. Do you believe that consenting adults have the right to meet their sexual needs in private?"

Shit. When he put it that way, my actions seemed downright un-American. Was he right? Was I buying into some sort of big brother-like censorship? I had to come up with a better defense for moral decency.

"I'd say yes, as long as it's not hurting anybody but give me a freakin' break, Dorian. Your business is to hurt people!"

"My business is to bring people pleasure."

"Bullshit. Disney World brings people pleasure."

He shook his head. "Forget it. You'll never understand."

Ivan chuckled from the front seat. "That's because she's a normal, my friend."

"Thank you," I said, gratefully.

"That wasn't meant as a compliment."

Now I hated both of them. I would have crossed my arms and pouted, except that I only had one arm and I was saving it to clock somebody if I had to.

Ivan, oblivious to my irritation, continued. "Do you think gays have the right to their lifestyle? Do you think the government should storm into their homes or bars and arrest them, simply for being gay?"

"Don't be stupid. It's not the same thing at all."

"And what about people who persecute them? Are they wrong?"

"If someone is beaten with a baseball bat for any reason, they should be punished."

At that point, Dorian piped up. "What about more subtle forms of discrimination, like denying a job to a homosexual or closing down a gay bar?"

Damn. I knew where this was going. "Dorian, your den of torture and depravity isn't the same thing as a gay bar and you know it."

"So it's okay to have gay clubs for people who live the gay lifestyle but not BDSM clubs for those who choose that lifestyle? Why?"

"Shut up." Not my most scintillating retort but I'd had enough of this conversation. I yawned. "You know? I think I'll just take a little nap. Wake me up when we get to wherever you're taking me—against my will."

* * * * *

I awoke with my cheek on Dorian's shoulder. The pressure of the seat against my back seemed to indicate the car climbing into the foothills. So many mountains surrounded the city of Las Vegas it would take the CSI team to find me.

I listened intently for any clues to determine our whereabouts. Nothing. Not a sound. I opened one eye to pitch darkness. We could be driving through deep space for all I knew. No, I'd be floating in zero gravity and as much as that sounded like fun, it was good to know we were somewhere on earth and probably still in Nevada.

The car turned and slowed to a stop. I yawned and stretched as if I'd just woken up, then I remembered I was mad at Dorian and yanked myself out of his grasp. Damn, now I had a super cold spot where his big, warm body had been. So it really did get cold in the desert at night. How would a Jersey gal know that?

"Time to get out, lover," Dorian said.

That damn, suede-soft voice of his turned me on all over again. What was wrong with me? Was I a nympho? I just wanted to jump his bones at every turn. As he opened his car door and got out, the drag on my arm reminded me that I had to scoot over to his side—either that or pull my cuffed arm out of its socket.

"Haven't you ever enjoyed the feeling of allowing your lover some freedom, knowing they'll stay because they want to—not because they have to?"

A look of surprise crossed his face. "Are you saying you'd stay with me because you want to?"

"No. Just curious."

He humphed—if that's a word. At any rate he made a noise that sounded like disappointment.

I probably should have minded my own business because after that he towed me a little roughly up to the front door of a well-hidden home. As Ivan unlocked it, he said, "Welcome to my hillside hacienda."

Holy Shit. As we entered the main home from the foyer, a large open floor plan revealed the size of the place. Travertine stone floors and one wall of solid rock gave it a semi cave-like feel. Some hacienda! Were all Doms stinkin' rich cavemen? The opposite wall of glass looked out over millions of glittering lights that could only be Sin City at night. If I had to be held hostage, this beat the heck out of a grubby warehouse.

"Thanks, man." Dorian clapped his friend on the shoulder and waited for him to set the alarm.

As I think I've said before, patience isn't one of my virtues. Hell, even virtue isn't one of my virtues. "So, asshole, are you going to unhook us now, or what?"

Dorian tucked his hand in his pants pocket.

Ivan's eyes bugged out. "Man, I know you like a challenge and everything but are you going to let her talk to you like that?"

"I've had to muzzle her before but it doesn't seem to do much good. I don't think she can be broken."

Broken? Housebroken? I know we had that whole dog discussion earlier but I thought it was metaphorical. "What the hell do you mean by that?"

The infuriating bastard didn't answer me.

Ivan continued their conversation as if I weren't even in the room. "Most subs aren't this mouthy even in the beginning. Are you sure she's worth it?"

Dorian laughed. "I'm not sure of anything where Faith's concerned."

"Wait just a minute. What are you two blabbering about? I'm not a sub. Never was and never will be." Just for emphasis, I slapped Dorian's shoulder. "And by the way, in case you didn't notice, I'm right here!"

Ivan shook his head. "I guess we'd better find Larry soon. I can't stand her abusing you much longer."

That struck me so funny, I burst out laughing.

"I'll have to stay here and watch her. Even though she can't escape, I'm sure she'll try. I don't want her fucking up your alarm system if she tries to disable it."

"Better you than me, buddy. Listen, make yourself comfortable. Larry can be hard to find when he doesn't want to be bothered by his fans. I might be gone a while."

"Who's Larry, anyway?" Larry the lounge lizard? That would be just what I needed.

"He's the hypnotist we've been looking for," Dorian said. "Although from the sounds of it, we might as well be searching for the Holy Grail."

"Oh, that's just awesome. So then what? Am I going to spend the rest of my life bound to you?"

He smiled, wryly. "Would that be so bad?"

Chapter Eight and a Half
Dorian's version

Another two minutes and I would have missed her escape. I'd done the best I could with what I had but obviously it hadn't been enough to hold her. I should have just taken her with me or had Ivan come straight to the room instead of meeting him in the garage but I'd wanted a few minutes alone with him to discuss my options. Beyond needing some peripheral help, I hadn't wanted to involve the other club owner any more than necessary. I was dealing with a cop, after all.

Thanks to Faith, my good intentions were once again blown to hell. We couldn't take her back inside, couldn't take her anywhere public and we had to get the hell out of there quickly in case we'd been caught on surveillance by security guards who weren't members of Ivan's club. Hey, I'd chosen that hotel for a reason.

The club itself was near too many landmarks, which left Ivan's home. No need to confirm we were headed there. I'd have done the same for Ivan had the situation been reversed.

True to form, Faith fell asleep, woke up, embarrassed me, then played twenty questions without the twenty limit. I sighed, I laughed, I got a boner.

Fuck. I fell further in love.

This was not a good thing. Ivan had said it best, even though "normal" was the last category I would ever stick Faith in. I had always pictured myself living the same life as my parents—vanilla on the outside, with a sharp bite smoothed by a creamy center. They had loved each other, loved the lifestyle, so much so that they had started the club where others could safely indulge their same fantasies. That was *normal*, dammit!

Faith didn't hesitate to show her sharp bite the second we entered Ivan's home. I understood that side of her. Hell, it got me hard every time, but she knew Ivan was also a Dom. Calling me an asshole in front of him was not her brightest moment. And that was saying a lot.

Chapter Nine
The beat goes on and on and on…

About five minutes after Ivan left, Dorian unlocked the handcuffs. Why he waited at all was beyond me. Maybe he didn't want to be embarrassed in front of the other Dom but he hardly seemed the type to worry about what other people thought.

I tried to rub the soreness out of my wrists. "How did you meet Ivan, anyhow?"

"We met at a conference here in Vegas."

I gasped. "You mean they have BDSM conferences?"

"Not exactly," he said and then he chuckled. "I was here for the pornography conference and awards."

Just when I thought he couldn't get any weirder. "You were a porn star?"

"Not me." He laughed again. "Someone I was dating."

"Date—Wait a minute." I shook my head, hard, trying to process this latest tidbit of information.

"I was young."

Still trying to digest this, I had to ask. "You date?"

At that point, he roared laughing.

"What?"

"I told you I dated a porn star and what do you pick up on? The idea of me, dating."

"Well… So, what was it like, knowing your girlfriend was boinking about a million other guys?"

His expression turned dark. "At first I thought I could handle it."

"But you couldn't?"

He shook his head. Walking into the kitchen, he signaled the end of that conversation. Just as well, it was triggering my *ick* factor. But I was hungry, so I followed him.

"So, what now?" I asked.

"Well, since it looks like we might be alone for a while, I thought maybe we could grab something to eat and then try a little more vanilla sex."

"Ha! You're not getting laid again until Hell freezes over."

He chuckled in his annoyingly superior way. "This is Vegas, blondie. I could make one phone call and get laid by a half dozen girls tonight if I wanted to."

I shrugged. "So go ahead. Do it."

He shook his head. "I hate to admit it but in a way, you were right about something."

"I was?" You'd think I'd respond to the part about vanilla sex but I had to know what I was right about, first.

Opening one of the cabinets, he located a jar of peanut butter and some crackers. "Part of the turn-on is that your partner could be elsewhere but chooses to be with you—free of charge."

"Oh." Knowing what he'd been through, it made sense that he might feel that way.

He prepared our snack and said, without ceremony, "I have to make a phone call. Be good while I'm gone."

He left the room and closed the bedroom door. A lot of good that would do him. I licked the peanut butter off the crackers so I could hear every word.

"Yeah, it's me. We might be stuck here for a little while. Larry seems to have gone underground."

Waiting...

"I probably could but there's no one else I'd trust to do this properly. I've seen what he can do."

More waiting...

"Forget it. I'm not going to hurt her."

Short wait and then a sigh.

"Look, you might as well know. I might be falling in love with her."

His short snort of a laugh, in response to something that was said, followed. Damn, I wish I could hear the other end of the conversation.

"Well, there's nothing you can do about that is there? I didn't exactly pick her as the ideal person to fall in love with. It happened and now everyone will just have to deal."

His cell phone clicked shut, cutting off whomever was on the other end.

My mind wandered through all the ramifications of what he'd imparted. Shit. He was falling in love with me. And I had admit the same thing was happening in my confused heart. A match made in Hell, as they say...

Speaking of Hell, now I'd have to measure up to a porn star? That was just friggin' awesome. What should I do? Wear stilettos and a smile when he comes home from work, then pretend he's the mailman?"

When he returned, he looked at my plate—specifically the crackers I'd licked clean and said, "Polly doesn't want a cracker?"

"I'd be eating lobster and caviar in Bermuda right now if it wasn't for you." I crammed a couple in my mouth at once and crunched. I'd never tasted anything so fantastic in my life but I still had questions so I mumbled around the sticky mush in my mouth. "Look, Dorian, about that sex…"

His face brightened. "Relax. I know what you're going to say."

"You do?"

"You're not always predictable but this time, yeah. You've changed your mind about Hell freezing over but you need to know one thing. And yes, I always wore condoms. I've been tested for STD's several times and I'm clean."

"Oh. Yeah. That's what I was thinking." It hadn't even occurred to me that he might have contracted HIV or HPV or Hep C. I was kind of ashamed that I hadn't thought about that yet. I would have—eventually.

As soon as he'd finished his own snack, he asked, "And you?"

"And me, what?"

"Have you always used condoms? Have you been tested?"

"Puleeease. I'm a cop, remember? That means yearly physicals and since I come into contact with blood and druggies, you better believe I get tested. And, I've never forgotten to wear a condom…er, you know what I mean."

Dorian grinned, grabbed me around the waist and

yanked me into his embrace, then he crushed me with both his arms and lips. *Fuck*. This relationship would be so much easier if I had some masochistic tendencies.

Chapter Nine and a Half
Open mouth, insert size thirteen shoe

Seriously, how was it possible for someone to be so lucky yet so unlucky all in the span of a couple of hours?

I was lucky I caught her trying to escape, unlucky in exposing Ivan. Lucky to fall in love, unlucky to have it be with someone who could never accept me. Lucky to have access to a hypnotist, unlucky to suddenly turn stupid.

Holy shit, had I really just mentioned to my lover that I'd dated a porn star? Way to turn a woman on, let alone a Jewish Princess cop.

"I was young," I threw out there, hoping that would somehow cover my gaff. I wasn't trying to apologize for my past, just for telling her about it.

She shook her head, which didn't bode well but once again she proved to be different from anyone I'd ever met, let alone slept with.

"You date?"

I couldn't help it—I burst out laughing. Unfucking-believable. I tell her I dated a porn star and what does she pick up on? The idea of me dating.

Still, this was Faith, so I waited for it. Sure enough, question gazillion and one followed and it was not a path I wanted to revisit.

"Well… So, what was it like, knowing your girlfriend was boinking a cast of thousands?"

I waited for the, *"And now I've slept with every one of those guys too, thanks a lot!"* that I was sure would follow, but the accusation didn't come and I found myself admitting to something I had never told a soul, including Sandy. "At first I thought I could handle it."

"But you couldn't?"

No and I wouldn't be able to handle question gazillion and three, either, so I walked away. Not far, just into the kitchen but there was no doubt the conversation was over. That had been a painful time in my life that I had let continue for way too long. After a year, I'd finally had to admit defeat. Sandy had been a nice girl and I really had cared for her but I couldn't get past constantly wondering how I measured up every time we slept together. Biased, I know but there it is.

I got Faith a snack and made a quick call to the club to check in. Unfortunately, Juliet answered the club's cell phone, which probably meant Guy was tied up. Literally. God knows what Juliet was doing to him in my absence. Not that I wanted to discourage her. Hell, I offered a standing bonus if they came up with something inventive enough to be passed on to clients.

I should have waited to make the call. I found myself mired in yet another conversation I didn't want to have and admitted my feelings for Faith to

Juliet, of all people. Yeah, I was still being stupid but what the fuck was it with women and their need to know everything ever said, done, or felt by the men in their lives?

That thought made me sad since I was only a temporary man in Faith's life. Our relationship was in the here and now and I wanted to fuck her right here, right now.

I went back into the kitchen and saw that she'd licked the peanut butter off the crackers I'd given her. Damn, I was really sorry to miss seeing that.

"Polly doesn't want a cracker?" I couldn't resist.

"I'd be eating lobster and caviar in Bermuda right now if it wasn't for you." She crammed a few in her mouth and talked around them. Somehow, she was still sexy. "Look, Dorian, about that sex…"

"Relax. I know what you're going to say."

"You do?"

Of course I did. I'd been expecting this part of the conversation since the moment I'd mentioned Sandy. It was a relief to tell her that yes, I'd always worn a condom. Every time I'd ever had sex to be specific, though I didn't go into that detail. Knowing Faith, she'd take that as an opening to ask how many times "every time" would be. While we were on the safe sex subject, I took the opportunity to throw in the inevitable STD conversation too.

Finally, my luck was back with me. We'd had the dreaded safe sex conversation and best of all, she hadn't denied changing her mind about having sex with me. I wasn't about to give her a chance to change it back.

I grabbed her around the waist and pulled her toward me, then kissed her to seal the deal. Oh yeah, we were going to have sex again all right. Only this time, we were going to add to our vanilla sundae.

Minus the cherry, thank God.

Chapter Ten
Faith discovers "Toys are us"

Getting naked as soon as we'd made it to the guest room, Dorian plunked his cute ass down on the satin coverlet and rummaged through the bedside drawer. "Let's see what kind of toys Ivan might keep for his guests."

"Toys?" I cried. "I thought you said we were going to have vanilla sex."

He pulled out a long, white, plastic dildo and held it up. "This is vanilla."

It looked cold and hard but not tasty at all to me. Every time I thought his sexual past could be redeemed, he went and did something like this to make me realize just how far from vanilla he was...and how I didn't even have any chocolate sprinkles on my soft serve.

His amber eyes had darkened and it looked like some flavor would seep into my life regardless of my lack of experience.

His cock bounced a little as he stood and turned

down the bed. I'm so glad I'd gotten my legs waxed and hadn't just shaved. They still looked smooth and I pictured wrapping them around Dorian's waist as he drove into me. Damn, my pussy pulsed for him. So where did he intend to put the dild...oh! No, he couldn't possibly think *that* was vanilla.

"No way in hell am I letting you use that thing. Not the way I think you might."

"Relax."

"I will not relax. In fact, I'll clench it so tight, you won't possibly be able to—"

He laughed so hard I thought he might wake the neighbors, if there were any.

"Don't worry. I think I know your limits but feel free to tell me if I don't." He shrugged. "You will anyway. Just keep in mind that I really do want you to enjoy the experience and I know you'll love this one."

"Fine but can't you just tell me what you're going to do?"

He kissed me, his lips sliding over mine with the same rhythm as his hand, feeling my breast. I reached out and grasped his impressive hard-on. His cock radiated heat, just as I sizzled inside everywhere our bodies rubbed together.

After making out for a few minutes, he got to his knees and straddled me. I was so mesmerized by the size of his cock, I'd forgotten all about the vibrator. I wrapped my hands around his hot staff and stroked from the bulging tip to his coarse, black curls. He reared back and closed his eyes as he moaned. Eventually, I let one hand do the work on his shaft while my other played with his balls. His hips pushed his cock in and out of my hand while my fingers teased his sac. A deep guttural sound emanated from his chest.

He blew out a breath and said, "Better let me focus on you for a while, Faith."

I clasped my hands behind my head, waiting to see what he'd do. If he went too far, I could push him off. Then he moved beside me and said, "Bend your knees."

Deciding to go along with just about anything he had in mind, trusting he'd stop if I objected, I did as he asked. He spread my bent legs as wide as they'd go and touched my folds gently.

"You're already wet for me."

"You sound surprised."

He smiled but said, "Not really." He ran his light touch over the ridges of my labia almost reverently. "Happy is more like it."

That's when I realized he *did* seem happy. For the first time since I'd met him, he lacked that tiger-like tension that suggested muscles ready to react at a second's notice.

His fingers swirled over the curls and creases, dipping in and out again while he gazed at my pussy. Groaning with the pleasure of his appreciation, I closed my eyes and lay back to enjoy it. My clit tingled, waiting for his finger to touch my tender button. Every now and then he'd barely graze it and I bucked to encourage more play there. At last his tongue took over and lapped my most sensitive flesh.

When I heard the buzz of the dildo I'd completely forgotten, my eyes popped open and I curled up just in time to see the rod enter my vagina. Then I was lost in sensation. He licked my clit while he fucked me with the vibrating toy. Its cool surface just emphasized how hot my cunt was. It slid in and out of my slick center easily. Between his insistent tongue going down on me and the vibration driving into me, it took no time at all before I responded and bucked into his mouth with a sudden, fierce climax. Electric sensations burst through my body like fireworks.

I thought he'd let up as soon as I stopped yelling his name but he didn't and the fluttering vibrations continued to assault my G-spot. Before I knew it, my body built up to another shattering peak. With my clit white hot, I wanted to weep, scream and tear out his hair. Instead I moved my hips to meet his rhythm and get the most out of this ride.

Whimpers, moans and noises I'd never heard before escaped my lips. The pleasure built to an almost intolerable level and I thought I'd turn inside out when my orgasm hit—again. Spasms of bliss ripped through me and radiated to every nerve ending while I cried out and shook uncontrollably. Honest to God, that earthquake could have toppled half the strip!

As I spiraled down, my body relaxed and Dorian eased the vibrator free. His fingers caressed my pussy sending little aftershocks out as a reminder of what he could do to me. Like I needed a memo.

When I could speak again, I said, "That felt wonderful but I'm afraid all of my muscles have turned into arm and leg shaped Jell-O."

"That must be why you taste like fruit cocktail." He licked all around his lips and grinned.

I grinned back but I wasn't kidding about my arm and leg muscles. I think my facial muscles were the only ones that worked. "I really can't move, Dorian. Can you give me a minute?"

"Of course," he said. He shifted his elbow up the

bed a little, then bent to lick and suck a taut nipple.

"No. I can't… No more… Please."

He chuckled. "Stop me." Kissing a trail across my cleavage, he nuzzled the other breast and sucked the tip into his mouth.

"Good God." After coming so hard—twice, I didn't think I'd be able to respond but my body didn't know when to quit. Clearly, I had to take matters into my own hands. I gripped his cock and squeezed. "It's your turn, now. Lie back."

He groaned and fell onto his back. His cock stood erect, waiting for my mouth.

Scooting down, I told myself, *I can do this.* If I didn't, my poor body would never get to rest. First, I licked the drop of liquid from the tip of his bulb and tongued the hole. He gasped. Okay. That wasn't too bad. Then I swirled around the shaft while he writhed and moaned.

Gratified, I went to work on his shaft, licking upward, slowly, as if it were an ice cream cone. Once I had thoroughly wetted his rod, I moved over the head and swallowed as much as I could before pulling back.

"Ah… That's the stuff, honey. I love a little cock worship."

Cock worship? Although I didn't care for the sound of that, arguing it now would ruin the mood. If it made him feel good, I'd let him call it whatever he liked. He could call it bowing to the vein-covered God and I'd ignore the chauvinism.

I started twisting the base as I massaged his length with my mouth. He groaned and pumped his cock in and out. His movements grew sharper and shorter and I knew he was nearing release. I stopped twisting and placed my thumb against the underside so that when he drew back, it pressed the sensitive spot under the head.

With a few frantic strokes, his body stiffened and I loosened my fist, releasing the pressure as he spurted cream into the air. Deep grunts accompanied his jerks. Some shot onto his abdomen and the rest drizzled down my hand. I rubbed and milked his cock until no more cum would come.

I watched his body relax even though his chest heaved. He lay there with his eyes closed so I let go of my death-grip and crawled up beside him. I was as pleased with myself as he was when he'd turned me inside out.

He gathered me into his arms and I snuggled close to him.

"Where did you learn to do that?" he asked.

"I just experimented a little. Did you like it?"

He turned his face toward me and opened his eyes. "Very much." We kissed for a few seconds and then drifted off to sleep.

Chapter Ten and a Half

Dorian eases her into his idea of topping

I always knew there were many facets of vanilla but was it too much to ask that if I fell in love with a vanilla woman, she would at least be at the French vanilla level? Christ. The dildo I chose wasn't even a jelly, or a two prong. Then she made it clear where she thought I was going to shove the thing and it was all I could do not to roll on the floor laughing. I mean, I absolutely intended to boldly go where apparently no man had gone before, just not at that moment. She needed time before she'd enjoy that particular dessert. Lots of time.

Once again, she'd annoyed me, surprised me, then made me laugh. Once again, I was so hard I wasn't sure I'd last long enough to add any flavor when plain felt so fucking good. But there we were, dildo in hand and I was determined to give some light play a try.

"Don't worry," I assured her. "I think I know your limits but feel free to tell me if I don't. You will anyway. Just keep in mind that I really do want you to enjoy the experience and I know you'll love this one."

She said something but I tuned it out after the word "fine" left her mouth. I had those soft lips under mine, a velvety nipple burning my palm and—oh shit!—my dick in her hand. I tried but I couldn't tune that out, even at the risk of unmanning myself on the sheets. Straddling her didn't help my control but it did distract me enough to realize what was going on. She was trying to get the last word in without speaking. No, she wasn't trying, she was succeeding. Then she was stroking my cock with one hand and my balls with the other and I figured I had no problem with her not saying another word all night. In fact, it would have been kinda nice...

As good as she'd look in a pearl necklace, I did stop her before that happened. There was another pearl to explore first.

Oh yeah. "You're already wet for me," I marveled. God, she was so slick and hot and soft it was all I could do not to bury my dick and shoot to the moon. But she'd made it clear she wasn't willing to land on Uranus and I really wanted to introduce her to Mr. Buzzjoy.

I had to face it, I was in heaven. I was exactly where I wanted to be and exactly with whom I wanted to be. It took every bit of control I had to remember to insert the dildo and man, was it worth it. She went absolutely crazy.

I brought her to supernova twice and would have gone for a third round but she had other ideas. I should have been prepared for that. Then again, nothing could have prepared me for the moment I felt and saw Faith Daniels go down on me with passion.

I heard my voice babbling something that made her pause and realized the words "cock worship" had somehow left my mouth. *Shit!* I wanted to apologize, being that I wasn't into the receiving side of pain but I could only groan with pleasure. Judging by the lustful, pain-free way she was going at me again, she'd forgiven me. The second I felt my dick start to throb against her hand, she showed me just how much I was forgiven and how much attention she'd been paying to where I liked to be touched.

I was going to come. I went into death mode— that final moment where my balls drew up and my mind automatically fought my body for control. I didn't know if that was what it felt like for every guy, just that I didn't feel it every time. Only when it was really, really intense.

Fuck, this one was going to kill me.

She eased up on the pressure and my mind lost the fight. Then I lost my mind. All I could do was grunt in ecstasy as I shot long and hard. Christ, if her hand hadn't been holding me steady, I would have been the one with the pearl necklace. She stayed with me, torturing me, caressing me, loving me until there wasn't a drop of cum left in my body.

Shit. She'd done it to me again. Would I ever have the upper hand with this woman? Even scarier, I was beginning to wonder if I ever wanted to.

I gathered her close and held on as we drifted off to sleep.

When I left with Ivan a few hours later, I felt pretty damn good about…everything. It was a crying shame it all had to come to an end but that was life. I was who I was and she was who she was. We weren't compatible in the outside world and I could only keep

her a prisoner in our little sex bubble for so long
before it burst.

Chapter Eleven
Faith seizes her opportunity

I awakened with a start and bolted upright. Something felt wrong. Alone in the bed, I listened for the sounds of frying bacon. Next, I inhaled deeply, hoping for the smell of fresh brewed coffee. Nothing. Not a sound in the whole house. Could I have been left alone?

Holy crap. Now's my chance! Determined to get the hell out of Dodge, I leapt out of bed and dressed as quickly as possible. So what if the door was locked. I was sure the adrenaline rush would help me pick up a good-sized chair and toss it through a window.

Rushing down the silent corridor in my stockings, I skidded to a stop in front of an unfamiliar brunette woman, seated crossed legged on the floor. She had something in her hand but it appeared too small for a gun.

"Good morning, Faith," she said. "I'm Nina."

"Ah—okay. What are you doing here? Where's Dorian?"

"Dorian and Ivan went out. I'm here to watch you."

"Watch me what? Wash behind my ears? Eat a decent breakfast? Brush and floss afterward?" I wished I hadn't thought of that. What if she *was* there to watch my every move? How annoying would that be?

"No. I don't need to watch you in the bathroom. There's no exit from there. I'm supposed to report anything you might do to escape, though."

Now I saw what she had in her hand. A cell phone. It looked exactly like Dorian's flashy status symbol. That would make sense since she probably knew Ivan's number and they'd probably have disabled the phones in the house. I'd have to be careful of what I said and did, apparently—so as not to arouse her suspicion. Then as soon as she relaxed, I'd give her the slip.

"I see. Well, I hope they went to get a big take-out breakfast," I said, stretching. I let out a yawn, hoping to look casual. "I'm starving this morning."

"No, they went to interview some possible client or employee or something. But if you're hungry, I can make you some breakfast. Do you like fried cornmeal mush?"

"Fried...what?" Hey, Toto, we're not in New Jersey anymore.

She got to her slippered feet. "It's delicious. You'll love it. Come into the kitchen with me."

"Whatever you say, lady." I guess I couldn't ask for a cake with a file in it—that might be considered unusual.

We made casual chit-chat as she pulled a loaf pan out of the refrigerator and began slicing pieces of

God-knows-what. It looked like mush that was no longer mushy. Then she pulled a frying pan from one of the cabinets and lathered it with butter. *Note to self. Frying pans kept in lower left cabinet.* You never know when you might need one to drop somebody.

Nina set the table and when the concoction was done, she smothered it with honey. *Another note to self. Honey is in the pantry.* Okay, so I hadn't tried sex with food yet. I was pretty sure Dorian would be up for that. He could call it cock worship but I'd call it a sugar addict's enthusiasm.

One bite and I was a Southwestern convert. This stuff beat the hell out of bagels and lox. Damn, it even trumped donuts!

Nina had set the cell phone on the counter and was about ten feet away from my chance to communicate with 911 as we ate. If I picked the right moment, I could distract her and grab it.

"So, are you and Ivan lovers?"

She actually blushed. "Not yet but I think it will happen soon."

"Yeah? What makes you think so?"

She lowered her eyes and pushed another bite of fried heaven into her mouth. I waited for her answer and eventually she got around to it.

"Ivan is my master but we're new to each other. We both need to build trust. I think that's happening."

I wondered if that's what Dorian meant when he said, "It's too bad we don't trust each other…" Did he think I was slave material? I almost laughed out loud but Nina was speaking again.

"I'm pretty sure he'll reward me with that pleasure soon."

Huh? Fucking as a reward? Then I had to admit I could see how that might work. So what the hell was Dorian rewarding me for? Trusting him a little and bitching at him any time I felt like it? Sounded like marriage to me. Strange man. I'd have to ask him—if I ever saw him again.

"So, is Ivan your first master?" I asked.

"No. I've had a few that didn't work out. I guess I was hard to tame."

If she was hard to tame, what was I? Suddenly feeling like a Tasmanian devil or recently captured lioness, I figured it was simply a matter of time before I mauled someone. I just hoped nobody had a dart gun.

"So is that what they call 'breaking' you?"

"Yes, exactly," she replied and smiled. Like I understood or something.

I shook my head and clucked my tongue. "It sounds like they broke your spirit."

Her posture straightened and she eyed me suspiciously. "What do you mean by that?"

Uh-oh. Dangerous territory. Don't make her reach for that cell phone, Faith. "I just meant that a relationship should be voluntary and mutual."

"Oh, it is! I want to give myself over to Ivan. I need that. And he needs me just as much."

Yeah, to boss around. "I see. So what do you need each other for?"

"Mutual pleasure, of course. And I'm happy to have someone else to make decisions for me. In my public life, I have to make a lot of decisions. Life or death decisions at times, and the responsibility overwhelms me."

I hadn't figured this woman for a life and death

decisions kind of gal. Now that she said that, I could kind of picture her in a white uniform. "But what if you don't agree with his decisions?"

"I can respectfully ask that he consider something else. He only wants what's best for me."

"Seriously? In my experience, men only want what's best for themselves."

"Perhaps you need to consider a different type of man?"

Different, huh? One thing I could say about Dorian—he was definitely different. But be that as it may, I wanted my freedom and I wanted it badly. I'd miss the best lovin' I'd ever had but hell, even Nina seemed freer than I was at the moment. Maybe in another life Dorian and I... Nah... Probably not.

"I have to visit the little girl's room," I said and stood.

"Oh, sure. You know where it is, right?"

It didn't matter because I wasn't really going there anyway. I was grabbing that cell phone and fighting my way out of that posh prison. Poor Nina looked as if she couldn't fight her way through a sale at Barney's.

I dashed for the counter and seized the cell phone, then I ran for the living room as fast as my stockinged feet would carry me. By the time she reached me, I had already pocketed the phone, picked up one of the modern metal chairs and charged toward one of the sidelights on either side of the glass front door. The door itself would be triple strength but those sidelights looked a little more vulnerable. With enough momentum and a battering ram like the back of that steel chair...

Smash! Alarms went off and I thought my ears

would explode. I turned sideways and managed to fit through the opening without impaling myself on any chunks of glass.

The shrill screams of Nina and the security system just made me run down the winding pavement faster. And, oh yeah, those stockings were going to run as fast as I did.

* * * * *

I hitchhiked my way back to the city limits and even managed to snag a ride to a police station on the outskirts. I thought I had it made. I couldn't have been more wrong.

"I need to see the captain," I said to the officer behind the bulletproof glass.

He barely glanced up from his newspaper. "He ain't here."

"Okay, so who's in charge?"

He slowly looked up, frowned at my disheveled appearance and said, "Who wants to know?"

"My name is Faith Daniels and I'm a police officer with the Waterloo, New Jersey, P.D."

"Waterloo, huh?" He snorted.

I didn't care for his attitude. I would have been nicer but he rubbed me the wrong way. Add to that sore feet, dirt, sweat and uncombed hair and suddenly my mood plummeted dangerously close to PMS territory.

"Well, Sergeant, how about if I just state my business?"

"Please do. I can hardly wait."

Not many people can outdo me when it comes to sarcasm. This guy had an attitude match coming. "It's too bad that your captain isn't available so I can report your rude ass but my more pressing complaint is that I need to report a kidnapping."

He sat up straight and his eyes widened as if he might be paying attention. He picked up his radio and said, "I'll call the lieutenant. Give me all the details you've got."

"Okay, I'm sorry if this is kind of sketchy but the two perps are calling themselves Dorian and Ivan."

"Last names?"

"I don't know."

"Description?"

"Both about six feet. Brown hair and eyes."

"What were they wearing?"

"I don't know."

He jotted down the names and then asked, "Any idea where they might be?"

"No."

Showing signs of exasperation, he raised his voice. "So, who's been kidnapped? Can you at least tell me that?"

"Me!"

He swore and smashed the expensive radio back down on the counter. "Look, lady. You don't look very kidnapped to me. You also don't look like a police officer. Now show me some ID or get lost and stop jerking my chain."

Damn it. I had no ID, of course. I hadn't had any ID on my person since my aborted wedding day. "Listen, can I make a phone call?"

He eyed me suspiciously.

"Come on… Hell, I'd get one if I were arrested."

"Don't tempt me."

Frickin' asshole. If only I could get behind the glass and ring his nasty neck, I'd be arrested and get my phone call, no questions asked. Fortunately the glass partition gave me a moment to think and I decided it wouldn't look good on my spotless record.

"Look, maybe you can make a call for me, collect. I can prove that what I say is true."

Wearing a snide expression, he asked, "Who do you want me to call? No one can identify you over the phone."

I threw my hands in the air. Then I remembered that someone could. Unfortunately, it was Roger. He had a nickname for me that no one else would know. It was kind of an embarrassing joke but it might work. I'm sure he'd want to know that I was okay—even as just a friend. And he could relay the information to my family, so it was worth a try.

"Look, my fiancé can verify that I am who I am by a password we chose in case we were ever in this situation. Then he can get in touch with my family and the department. They need to know I'm alive, for crissakes!" Jews didn't usually use that expletive but he didn't need to know I was Jewish—just pissed.

He narrowed his eyes, skeptically. "In case you were ever in this situation?"

Okay, I'd be skeptical too in his place. "Look it's not so much a password as it is a private nickname he gave me that no one else would know. Trust me, if this wasn't an emergency, I wouldn't tell you about it."

He shook his head but picked up the phone. I gave him the number, which he wrote down. Then he glanced up at me, expectantly, with the pencil still hovering over the paper.

"And the nickname?"

Holy crap. In any other situation I'd rather die than tell anyone Roger's pet name for me but given the circumstances, I had little choice. I took a deep breath and spat it out. "He called me, My Little Potato Knish."

"What the hell is that?"

"It's a potato dumpling."

He dropped the pencil and gave me a funny look. "Jesus! He may as well have said you have a fat ass!"

I felt the heat of a furious blush rise to my cheeks. "What?"

He shook his head and laughed at my expense. I folded my arms and turned my back so I wouldn't have to endure his amusement while I waited for him to compose himself.

That took quite a while. Eventually he calmed down and made the call. I thought he was going to crack up all over again when he told the person-to-person collect call operator that Roger had a call from his potato knish.

We both waited in silence. Then the sergeant hung up and turned to me. "He's never heard of you. Sounds like you got dumped, dumpling."

So much for the concern of an old friend.

Chapter Eleven and a Half
Dorian learns a few things

Great. Ivan and I had located Larry the Hypnotist. In fact, we were sitting in the guy's driveway. Only he'd left town again, for a gig in Georgia. My choices were now severely limited because there was no way in hell that Faith would willingly drink anything I handed her before boarding a plane for Georgia, as in the former USSR.

Could I trust her enough at this point to simply let her go?

"You're not letting her go." Ivan said.

Great. Either Ivan was a mind reader, or I'd become a transparent Dom. The former wasn't likely and the latter didn't bode well for my profession.

"Do you like what you do for a living, Dorian?"

"What kind of a question is that? I'm damn good at what I do!" I turned toward him and gave him my best glare but he didn't so much as flinch. Of course, he wasn't some sub defying his master. He was a Dom who ran his own club.

Except the look on his face had nothing to do with the game. This was a friend being honest with a friend.

"Being good at it doesn't mean you like it," he calmly pointed out.

Shit. I felt the jolt of the nail hitting the head. The lifestyle was fine with me. Hell, I enjoyed it but it wasn't something I'd really chosen for myself. I had been born into it and I had become bored with it long before Faith barreled down the wrong aisle.

She'd cured my boredom both in bed and out.

For the first time since my parents had died, I found myself questioning my ability to make the right decision. For the first time in my adult life, I turned to someone else and asked, "What do I do now?"

"You finish what you started," Ivan said without a hint of indecision. "You find another hypnotist to do the job. She's a cop, Dorian. She'll never accept the club for what it is and there are people who rely on you, some of them for their very livelihood. When you've seen this through, then you go back and make the decision to continue on or not."

I got what Ivan was saying. Faith wouldn't remember me but I'd know who she was and could approach her as vanilla if that was the life I chose.

"Let's find out who might be the second best hypnotist in Vegas and get this over with."

Ivan started the car and we headed back to his house to do some research. He didn't say much, which was fine with me. I had a lot to think about, as it was and I still intended to slip another round of cock worship in before Faith's mind got wiped. I had no problem teaching her what I liked all over again but God knows, any plan that involved her wasn't predictable.

By the time we pulled into Ivan's driveway, I knew it was going to be fuck first, research later. There was only one problem.

Faith was gone.

The front door was wide open but as we got out of the car and approached, it became clear that she'd escaped by smashing the glass next to the door. Expensive glass, apparently. Ivan hadn't stopped cursing since we'd pulled up. Then we caught sight of Nina cowering in the corner of the living room. One look at Ivan's face and I began to wonder if she should have gone with Faith.

I also had to wonder why I wasn't worried that Faith was on the loose.

"Kneel." Ivan ordered Nina before us.

The poor girl did as she was told, trembling with fear. "I—"

"You dare to speak without permission?" Ivan roared, effectively cutting her off. "You'll get twenty lashes for that alone and each word you use when I say you can speak will be worth one more. If you don't call me Master, it will double."

Brilliant. The true terror left the room the second Nina realized that Ivan wasn't going to send her packing. As Ivan barked out the questions he wanted answers to, the atmosphere became charged with the sexual excitement that could only be generated by a Dom and sub who were true mates. I wondered if either or both of them knew that yet.

"Did the alarm go off?"

"Yes, Master."

"Did the police come?"

"No, Master."

"Why didn't you call us?" I threw in.

"She took your phone."

Nina didn't dare look up from Ivan's shoes but if she had, she would have caught the calculating smile he shot me. Like I couldn't tell he was enjoying this by the erection threatening to burst his zipper and jump down Nina's throat.

"Ten lashes for not calling me sir too," I helpfully added. "Why didn't you call your Master's cell?"

A few seconds passed while she tried in vain to keep the word count down. "About to, sir. Came home."

"Strip and spread yourself across the horse in the playroom for your forty-three lashes," Ivan commanded. "I'll be deciding when, where and with what."

"Yes, Master."

"Forty-five."

Nina ran for the door to the basement, stripping her clothes off on the way.

"That do anything for you?" Ivan asked, brow raised.

"Fuck you. Would it be doing as much for you if it were Faith you were about to punish? Being that Nina is your soul mate and all."

The truth slammed into Ivan so hard he actually reeled a bit. Then he cursed, cursed some more when the truth didn't go away, then he strode to the basement door with a hissed, "Go. Find. Her."

I wasn't worried for Nina. If anything, the tent in Ivan's jeans had grown, and it wasn't like I had to advise him not to give all forty-five lashes at once. He knew what he was doing. Besides, I had my own worries.

As if on cue, Ivan's cell, which was indeed on the carpet near the couch, announced a text message. I did think about getting Ivan but the familiar crack of leather on skin, the familiar whimper of pained ecstasy drifted up the open stairwell. Ivan was busy.

I viewed the message. Sure enough, it was from a security guard at the hotel. Faith had just been seen on camera.

I heard a deep, masculine groan of pleasure after the first ten count and knew Ivan would be busy for a while, so I grabbed his keys and made off with his car. I did leave the gift I'd gotten Faith on the counter, figuring Nina deserved it. I didn't know what I was going to say or do to Faith. I just knew I had to get to her. Damn it, what little time we had left wasn't going to be spent apart.

Chapter Twelve
Faith feels faithless

I'd hitched one last ride back to the strip. The driver gave me the willies, so I had him let me out at a bus stop. It was near the hotel I'd stayed in the night before last. I'd gladly walk the rest of the way. I hoped the concierge would help me more than LVPD. And if Dorian hadn't checked out yet, perhaps I could order a much-needed stiff drink and charge it to the room.

I walked into the lobby, as bold as brass and hoped no one would object to my bare feet. I had those black high-heeled pumps and hoped I could get them back along with the little black dress I had abandoned in the parking garage. The silk scarves could rot in the shower for all I cared.

Luck was finally with me. Dorian had not checked out yet so while someone from the staff scurried off to see if my clothing bag had landed in lost and found, I waited in the bar for the concierge.

It's amazing what a good hotel will do for their

guests. I just prayed my lack of shoes didn't send a red flag that signaled I'd lost everything but my blue cami and ivory pencil skirt, gambling. I should have said, it's amazing what a good hotel will do for *paying* guests and high rollers.

While sipping my umbrella drink, courtesy of Dorian's tab, I had quite a while to think. There were other phone calls I could make but I didn't want to use Dorian's cell phone for that. I didn't know if he had a tracer on it and it might be nice to hit redial at some point since I think he called the club last.

It's funny that I didn't think to have the cops call the hotel for Dorian's last name. There couldn't be too many Dorians staying there. My class in Freudian Slips 101 indicated that I might not want him arrested, after all. Even with the restraints, kidnapping and plot to wash my brain, I still dug him. I could have met a very different fate if not for his intervention. And weirdest of all, he was falling in love with me. Well, maybe that wasn't the weirdest thing but it was up there.

I pulled his cell phone from my pocket and stroked it as if, somehow, he'd know how much I would miss him. I'd never fallen in love with someone and they with me at the same time. I may have told myself I loved Roger but on some level, I knew I was merely hoping I did—or would at some point in the future. Fat chance.

Did I mention Roger was a lazy lover? Yeah. Even without a crystal ball I could predict I'd be the one on top for the rest of my life. Or as Dorian calls it, "The Top". I liked sharing the partner on top position to be honest. I liked sharing Dorian's bed. Sharing his smiles. Sharing his money...oh that was crass, huh?

Oh well. I had to admit his tab was coming in handy. "Yes, bartender. I'll have another one of these, please."

As a good bartender without much business at the moment, he answered my request right away. As he placed the third umbrella drink in front of me, he asked, "Man trouble?"

"How did you know?"

"You just have that look."

"What look?"

"Like your dog ran away. Only you don't look the type to own a dog."

Sheesh, this guy was good. "Well, you're almost right. Except I'm the one who ran away."

He polished some clean glasses and continued the conversation. "It's all the same. So what did he do? Cheat on you?"

"No," I said, wondering why I was about to pour my heart out to a complete stranger.

"Oh no. He beat you, didn't he? I should have guessed. You do look a little roughed up."

"Now wait a minute. He'd never do that. He could have done a number on me plenty of times, he's strong as an ox but he didn't. I did this all myself. For your information, I crashed through a plate glass window, ran down an asphalt road in my stocking feet, hitchhiked back to the hotel and here I am."

Incensed, I took a big gulp of my drink and began coughing.

"Sorry," he said and rushed off to fetch me a glass of water. "You okay?"

Eventually I stopped sputtering. "Yeah. I'm peachy."

"Look, I didn't mean to pry. You just looked like

you needed to talk."

I shrugged. "Don't worry about it. You were just doing your job."

I set the alcohol aside and sipped the water in dainty little swallows. The bartender noticed another customer who had just landed on the other side of the bar and thankfully, he left.

Meanwhile, I continued my pity party and wondered where the concierge had gone. Or, more importantly, how long I'd have to wait until he returned. As I pouted, I felt something. You know those prickles that travel up your spine and the back of your neck when you know someone is looking at you? I had those. Maybe the concierge had noticed my bare feet.

I glanced around, surreptitiously. There in the doorway, hands in his pressed pants pockets, stood Dorian—studying me with the saddest look on his face. I can't describe what came over me. I should have run again, yet he pulled me in with his eyes and relief flooded over me—he'd found me. When had he become everything I wanted?

I hurried over to him and launched myself into his arms. He caught me and held on so tight my bare feet didn't touch the floor. As he spun me around, I caught the bartender's smile. Yup, he got to see a lot of train wrecks in his line of work but probably didn't witness too many happily ever afters. I decided to give them both the full thrill. Leaning back, I said, "Thank God you came after me. I've changed my mind—about everything."

"You don't hate me anymore?"

"Absolutely not. I love you."

He almost dropped me. But to his credit, without

much of a gap, he dipped his head and kissed me on the lips.

* * * * *

In the elevator, on our way upstairs, I thought about what the word *everything* might imply to him. I hoped he didn't expect me to become submissive because that wasn't going to happen. Every now and then he'd glance down at me and smile with a combination of lust and victory in his eyes. Oh boy, we needed to talk.

"Um, Dorian, you know that everything didn't mean *every*thing, right?"

He sighed. "I knew it was too good to be true."

"Well, hang on. Let's get to the room so we can figure this out."

He shrugged. "I understand. Love is rarely unconditional and you still don't trust me."

That sounded so wrong. I felt as if I had given him a gift and then taken it back. I wouldn't let my Jewish guilt turn me into someone I wasn't, though—and he still hadn't told me he loved me back. What was that about? Macho pride? Screw that.

As we approached the door to our room, he squeezed my hand and winked. Okay, maybe he was saving it for the right moment. Maybe he wanted to yell it out during sex. Vanilla sex, thank you very much. Just because I'm a woman didn't mean I had to make all the compromises.

He held the door open for me and I tried to plan what I was going to say. *It's not that I don't trust you—it's just that I don't TRUST you.* No, that wouldn't help at all. Sheesh, I hadn't thought I'd be doing this so deciding how to approach the topic had never entered my mind.

Fortunately, he spoke first. "I think we can make this work."

Whew! I sat on the chair in the corner so I wouldn't jump his bones and said, "I'm glad you feel that way. Tell me how."

"Well, obviously I can't expect miracles. You're not the whips and chains type but I do expect to be treated fairly. With respect. A little admiration would be nice too."

Admiration, huh? Well, I did admire his taut abs, broad shoulders and perfect butt. I doubted that was what he meant, though.

"And," he continued, "You can trust me. I think you know that deep down."

He was right. My gut said that he'd never purposely hurt me—and a cop's gut feelings are pretty dependable. "I'm beginning to feel better about putting my trust in you. Keep talking."

"I think it's your turn to talk." He sat on the edge of the bed looking all gorgeous and tempting.

My mouth watered. But okay. Here was my chance. "I need to know how you feel about me."

"Isn't it obvious?"

"I want you to say it. Isn't it nice to hear it, out loud?"

He smiled and nodded. "Yes, it is."

My heart fluttered expectantly as he sauntered over and leaned on the arms of my chair. An expression of both momentous import and sincerity temporarily halted my breathing. He held my gaze and a golden glow materialized within his amber brown eyes.

"I love you, Faith."

Oh, melt me and lick me off the chair! Quivers effervesced from my spine to my heart. He loved me too! A stupid tear formed in the corner of my eye. Since I couldn't count on my ability to form coherent thoughts or words any more, I tried to look like a temptress and crooked my index finger at him.

He smiled like the cat that found the cream. Come to think of it, the space between my thighs had dampened considerably.

"Come to bed," he whispered, softly.

It seemed right to seal the sentiment with lovemaking, yet there had to be more issues to work out. *Forget that.* I needed him. Wanted him. And as long as he wanted me too and we were both prepared for some differences between us. We'd figure it out.

Chapter Twelve and a Half
Confession is good for the body and soul

When I arrived at the hotel, I was wondering how I was going to find her when I swear to God, I sensed her near me. Sure enough, when I followed that instinct, it led me to her. Figured she'd be in the bar.

She must have sensed me too because I'd only been watching her for a minute when she turned and saw me. She was going to run. An overwhelming feeling of loss hit me when she slid off the barstool and then she did run. Right into my arms.

When she finally pulled back, she said exactly what I'd wanted to hear. "Thank God you came after me. I've changed my mind—about everything."

"You don't hate me anymore?"

"Absolutely not. I love you."

Jesus. There was nothing I could do but kiss her. At least, not until we got up to our room. Only she went all, "let's talk about it" on me in the elevator.

"Um, Dorian, you know that everything didn't mean *every*thing, right?"

I sighed. "I knew it was too good to be true."

I tried to take it from there, to say whatever the hell it was she was looking for before we got to the room but it didn't work. We went back and forth about trust a bit but she still wasn't satisfied, so I still wasn't getting laid. It wasn't until I put the conversation back on her shoulders that she finally spelled out what it was she needed.

I had no problem giving it to her. "I love you, Faith."

After that, she had no problem giving it to me.

Chapter Thirteen
Mind blowing

Naked and between the sheets, he kissed me for all he was worth. I mean without any loss of contact, he managed to nip, lick, swirl and suck my breath away. I lost myself in his loving lips. Had we stayed just like that, just kissing all afternoon, I'd still have been happy.

But as soon as he fondled my breasts, I anticipated some amazing sucking and fucking and, thrilled beyond reason, more moisture leaked from my eager primal core.

He squeezed my nipples, gently at first and then with more pressure. Excitement built quickly. His hand slid toward my mons and I arched into it as his mouth took possession of my breasts. Sucking my nipples the way he had squeezed them, sent ripples of need straight to my clenching center. Even with his hand just resting over my pussy, I craved his cock inside my heat.

And then his magic fingers began to move.

Dear God. I needed release. I needed to climax right into his mouth. I needed to feel every thrust of his cock. Speaking of his cock...

I reached for the beautiful instrument of my pleasure but he pulled away and it slid right through my fingers.

Confused, I asked, "What's wrong?"

"I'm saving him for something special."

Him? I wondered if "he" had a name but decided not to ask. I'd heard of guys who named their cocks. Well, something other than Dick, Peter or Rod, that is. I wasn't sure if I wanted to know *its* name. For God's sake, it's not like I've named my boobs or my vagina. What the hell would I call them? Bobbie, Melanie and Virginia? No way.

"So what did you have in mind for...something special?"

"I want another mind-blowing blowjob. It's not like you couldn't swallow if you—"

"Oh here we go again with the assumption that a J.A.P. can't or won't give a good blowjob or swallow. Well, lie back, honey, because I'm gonna blow your brains out."

His eyebrows rose but instead of rewording what I'd said, I pushed him onto his back. He must not have been too afraid since he clasped his hands behind his head and waited.

"First of all, it really depends on the way you feel about a guy. If you love every nook and cranny of a man, you can touch him just about anywhere and not be too grossed out. I'll bet that most women just aren't over the moon about their guys. Five minutes ago, I'd have faced a firing squad for you. Now, I'm losing the mood. I don't want sex to be about proving myself."

He reached out and drew me to him. Cupping my cheek, he said, "I didn't mean it to sound like that. You drive me wild—in and out of bed—but with a few moves that I can teach you…"

"Yeah? What?"

"You could make me your sex slave." He grinned.

It was so ironic, I had to laugh. Of course his boyish grin went straight to my loins.

As if I did it for a living, I reached for his erection with confidence. Placing my mouth around the bulb, I bathed it with saliva and twirled my tongue around. He let me know I was on the right track with an appreciative, "Mmmm…" I loved earning his approval—at least in this area.

I tried to release the burden of having to measure up to the women in his past. I didn't know how many there had been, how skilled they were and I didn't want to know. I just knew that I wanted to pleasure my lover and stop worrying about things I couldn't change.

Sure, maybe there were things he could teach me but I hoped to show him that my baseline knowledge might be better than expected. With luck, I could take the same pleasure in giving as I always felt while getting. Well, okay. Those two things weren't exactly the same and never would be but Dorian's sexual fulfillment was important to me. I decided the best way to do that would be to lose the inhibitions and just go for it.

I flicked the head with my tongue a few times and followed the shaft down all the way to the root, licking and flicking. When I reached his bare ball sac, he writhed under me and let out an animated moan.

Believe it or not, I was having fun. Opening wide, I tried to take his generous scrotum into my mouth.

"Whoa, watch the teeth, darling."

Yeah, that didn't work. I wasn't one of those lucky girls who could fit a fist in her mouth. I'd need a flip-top head for that.

So I returned to licking my way around each testicle in a figure-eight pattern and he groaned in bliss. Hey that was pretty good and I'd just made it up. So I let my imagination roam free and tried anything and everything I thought might feel good to him. Moans, groans, grunts and gasps brought instant gratification. Mine, not his.

At one point he murmured something so unusual, I wasn't sure I'd heard him right. It sounded like, "Mmm…never thought vanilla could taste like this." Score one for the subtle, discriminating taste of vanilla!

When I had built up to hard, deep suction, he made it clear that whatever he was penetrating in about five seconds was going to get a bath. Uh-oh. Decision time.

What should I do? Hang on and see if I could tolerate the taste of cum or stop and grab a condom? Fortunately or not, the decision had already been made. He trembled and jolted into my mouth, spurting his hot liquid.

Now I was faced with another decision. Spit or swallow? I'd never done this before but I'd be damned if I'd admit it. Besides, this wasn't the time to stop and ask. Cum just kind of naturally ran out the sides of my mouth and down his cock while he continued to jerk with aftershocks. His hands were wrapped around my hair, possibly to hold it out of the way of the dripping mess running over both sides of his abdomen.

When I'd wrung him dry, he lay still. I rose up on my hands and knees to gauge his reaction. An expression somewhere between awe and wonder colored his face. Well, a flush colored his face but the awe and wonder seemed to add to the glow.

I wasn't sure if I wanted to look smug or jump up and down on the mattress. He was certain to have experienced this before but part of the turn-on for him had something to do with suspecting I hadn't. So I simply smiled.

He reached for me. I rolled into the space that I now thought of as mine. Head on his shoulder, free hand resting on his chest. He cupped my head and stroked my hair without saying a word. Then he kissed my forehead and said, "That was good."

Good? That's all? *Just good?* What did I have to do to blow this guy's mind? A shudder passed through me as I thought about it.

"Is my vanilla princess cold?" He pulled the top sheet over us just as I struck him in the chest.

Chapter Thirteen and a Half
Another dare

I couldn't help testing her trust. Or pushing her boundaries. Hey, the Dom in me wasn't going to go away overnight, right? And I still needed to get everything I could before she blanked on who I was and the things we'd done together in bed.

So we made out for a while but when she reached for my dick, I pulled away and let her know I had something else in mind.

"I want another mind-blowing blowjob. It's not like you couldn't swallow if you—"

Oh yeah. She pushed me onto my back but instead of swallowing my dick, she made me swallow my words. I had to do some fast backpedaling to get what I wanted but oh man, it was worth it the second she guided my cockhead into her mouth. She actually licked my balls too, driving me crazy until she got me with her teeth. She quickly went back to licking and I went back to heaven.

I didn't try to hold back and it wasn't long before I

felt that tingle at the base of my spine. Would she really let me come in her mouth? Could she do it? It wasn't without risk on my part, either, considering the damage she could do. Surprise was never a good thing during that vulnerable moment.

She started sucking hard again and the choice was out of my hands. I wrapped my fingers in her hair and held on for dear life as I exploded in her mouth. Ah, God, the added heat caused another burst down her throat and she took that too.

She'd not only done it, she was good at it. But when I tried to tell her that and snuggle up for some recovery time, she freaked out on me!

Chapter Fourteen
Faith's lesson in respect

The next thing I knew, I lay flipped onto my stomach with my hands pinned over my head.

"That wasn't very nice. I thought we agreed to respect each other," he grumbled.

"For the love of God, Dorian, what do you want from me? I just gave you everything I had! And you say, 'that was good'?"

"What's wrong with that? It *was* good. It was very, very good. I enjoyed your special attention, tremendously."

I sighed. Would there ever come a time when I didn't wind up immobilized before, during or after sex with this man? He loosened his grip but didn't let go.

"What's wrong, Faith?"

I lay there, wondering what to say. That I was jealous of the other women who came before me? That I thought everyone he'd ever slept with knew more about sex than I did? Hmm... Do you think I was feeling a tad insecure? Yup, you betcha.

"Look, I know this sounds pathetic but there's so much you've experienced that I never will. I'm ten years older than you but you've probably had more sex than bunnies on a rabbit farm. I don't know if I'm enough for you."

He laughed and let go. I rolled up on one elbow and stared at him. I'd think twice before I hit him again but I still didn't see anything funny about the situation.

"You're more than enough for me, sweetheart. You've stirred something in me I can't quite put my finger on. I've thought about us—a lot. I want to be with you in a different way than I've ever been with a woman before and it unnerves me."

"You? Unnerved? You're kidding."

"No, I'm not. I… I could a…"

Hmm… I guess I did throw him off balance. But I wanted to know exactly what he was afraid of. Sure, I'm a cop but he never let that bother him. If it did, we wouldn't be in this situation.

"What are you struggling to say, Dorian?"

He let out a big breath with a whoosh and his gaze dropped to his lap. I wasn't about to let him off the hook, though. So I sat there silently while he put a few words together and got them out of his mouth.

"Look… What I'm trying to say is that I wouldn't mind spending the rest of my life trying to figure you out and that makes me very nervous."

Huh? Did I hear that right?

"I even bought you a present while I was out trying to find the guy who could help us."

"You bought me a present?"

"Yes but when we got back to Ivan's and I found

you gone, I left it for Nina. She was so traumatized, she needed a little comforting."

"Why on earth was *she* traumatized? I was the one who bashed through the plate glass window."

"She was afraid Ivan would punish her and he did. I saw her panic and cower from him at first. That's not what I want. Then I thought about how you'd behave if the situation were reversed." He laughed.

"What's so funny?"

He shook his head. "My visual. I saw you running after her with a dustpan and brush demanding she clean it up."

"Hell yeah. And call the nearest glass company to come out and…"

He leveled his intelligent gaze at me.

"Uh-oh. You left the glass right where it was, didn't you."

"Yes."

"Damn."

"I think your idea of calling a glass company is also a good one."

"I'll call but you should pay for it. I wouldn't have been in that stupid situation if not for you."

He hesitated but acknowledged the truth with a short nod.

It seemed as if we were able to compromise, after all. Once that was settled, my mind immediately returned to something else of importance.

"So what was the present you bought for me but gave to Nina?"

He shrugged. "It wasn't anything big. Just kind of an inside joke. It was a candle in a glass jar—vanilla spice scented."

"Awww…" He might as well have said he got me

a puppy.

He trailed one finger up my arm and electricity sizzled everywhere he touched. "I think someone needs to get laid first and then we can go back to Ivan's."

"Uh-huh? And who would that be?"

"You, darling." His finger traveled to my chin and he drew my face close to his. "Even when you're supposed to be relaxing you're as taut as a coiled spring."

"Am not."

Without getting into a childish rendition of "are too, are not" he bridged the short gap to my lips and kissed me utterly senseless. He trailed his lips over to my ear, where he nibbled, then continued kissing his way down my neck to my cleavage. Of course, he painstakingly pleasured my breasts only this time he didn't just cup my mons. He ran his fingers over ridges and between the folds, finally burying two fingers inside me. My core clenched. Oh yeah, we were headed to orgasm central and I couldn't wait.

Dorian backed down the bed, slipped his agile body between my legs and held each ass cheek in his splayed fingers. The predatory look he gave me right before he feasted on my pussy made me want to slide onto a silver platter. I barely felt him massage my gluteus muscles as he licked my clit. *Oh, God.* I quivered as familiar tingles signaled my impending bliss.

I did something I'd never done before and didn't know why I was doing it then. I cupped and squeezed my own breasts. I pinched my nipples just as he sucked my nubbin and climaxed as if shot out of a cannon. Heated liquid gushed. My convulsive orgasm would have crushed his fingers had they still been inside me. As powerful as any I'd had, I rode the wave all the way to my last whimper. He waited until I'd come back to Earth before he spoke.

"My turn again," he said.

Gloriously satisfied, I throbbed but couldn't move. "Uh-huh." *Pant, pant.* "In a minute." *Pant, pant.*

He smiled in understanding. "Stay where you are," he said.

"No problem." *Pant, pant.*

He donned his condom, grabbed two fluffy pillows and wedged them under my butt. This had to be the most overextended pelvic tilt I'd ever been in but I was in no shape to complain. He parted my legs and positioned himself on his knees between them.

"Faith, I want you to watch me fuck you. I think you'd agree I'm someone who does what he wants, especially in the bedroom."

I nodded.

His tip prodded my opening. "I choose who I fuck, Faith." Plunging inside, his cock stretched my channel and penetrated all the way to the thick hilt. *Ahhh...* With his hands resting on my knees, he began a slow, tortuous rhythm. "Watch me fucking you, Faith."

I did. I gazed at his cock as it sank into me where we joined. It was as if I'd never seen this before. Truthfully, I probably hadn't. It's hard to see anything in the dark with eyes scrunched shut.

"See how I pull partway out but push my cock in again. I choose to *be* with you. I want to be joined with you. *You,* Faith. I'm inside *you.* I'm fucking *you.*"

"Oh, God," I squeaked and looked up into his evocative gaze.

He increased his rhythm. "Pay attention to me too, Faith. I want you to watch us fucking. I want to know you want me too."

Remembering that I needed to participate, I rocked my hips to meet his thrusts but also did as he instructed. I watched us fucking. It was hands down the most intimate experience I could remember having and I burned the image into my memory banks. His heavily lidded eyes moved from our coupling to my face. He smiled and returned to watching our bodies meet.

"You want me, then," I said idiotically.

"I want you. Over and over and over."

He didn't treat me like an idiot. As I thought about it, I realized he had never treated me as a know-nothing, sexually challenged, moron—ever.

"I want to hear you tell me you want me. You want this." His soft as suede voice practically caressed me.

"I do want you—and this!"

He closed his eyes with a satisfied smile and increased the tempo, pumping into my lucky sheath. Adding a finger rub over my nubbin clinched it. He set off my orgasm as if he'd pressed the big, red, launch button. I shook, spasmed and screamed. With all the pillows under my ass, I had nothing to muffle the noise as I cried out but I couldn't help it. The onslaught on my sensitive nerve endings grew to mind-boggling proportions. I couldn't think. Couldn't control my body. All I could do was feel and react.

Dorian had apparently succumbed to his own stimuli. His body jolted several times and heat flooded my core. His face mixed agony and ecstasy into one beautiful portrait of a satisfied man until he collapsed beside me.

"By the way, don't forget to return my cell phone that you swiped."

Oopsy. "On one condition."

"What's that?"

"Tell me your last name."

He laughed. "It's Markoff."

Chapter Fourteen and a Half
Dorian's feelings come out

She hit me! Over a freakin' compliment!

I had no choice but to immobilize her and try to figure out what was going on in that fascinating female brain of hers. Jesus. I tell her she needs work on her blowjob skills and she sets out to prove me wrong. I tell her she's good at it and she hits me!

I knew there had to be more to it but I wasn't getting any answers. Then she sighed, which was almost as bad as hearing the word, "fine". I was definitely screwed, so I figured I should just bite the bullet and get it over with.

"What's wrong, Faith?"

She didn't say anything for a while and when she did speak up, it was the last thing I expected from her. She was feeling insecure. Faith. Insecure. About having sex with me. I couldn't help it—I started laughing. She, of course, didn't hit me when she should have.

That was Faith. *My* Faith.

I knew then that was exactly the sentiment she was looking for but man, it was as hard as hell to spit something like that out without sounding like a dork. Besides, didn't "I love you" cover all the bases? Guess not.

Okay, I could do this. "Look... What I'm trying to say is that I wouldn't mind spending the rest of my life trying to figure you out and that makes me very nervous."

She didn't look convinced. Maybe if I'd actually looked at her while I said it...but it was too late now. I'd said it and I was done.

There was only one thing that would derail my lady's train of thought. I had to bring out the big guns. "I even bought you a present while I was out finding the guy who could help us."

Oh yeah, worked like a charm. So did convincing her she was still owed an orgasm. This was good. Not only was I going to get laid, I could show her how special she was to me at the same time.

I started out right, taking my time with her glorious tits and fingering her sweet pussy before I worked down to settle my chest between her spread legs. Beautiful. I grabbed her ass and held on tight as I dived in. She wasn't going anywhere for a while.

The plan was to bring her total orgasmic meltdown, then thrust into her and start the process all over again. I could have pulled it off if I hadn't looked up to get off on her reaction. What I saw blew my mind. She was squeezing her own tits, her long slim fingers pinching those ripe berry nipples.

My sweet vanilla girl was beginning to lose her inhibitions.

I kept my eyes on her and licked her clit out of its

hood, then sucked it between my lips. She went wild and I dug my fingers deeper into the curves of her lush ass and held on. Her tits were bulging between her spread fingers, her nipples looking like they'd burst from her pinching pressure as she screamed my name. In that moment, I swear I felt her clit convulse and explode against my mouth.

It was all I could do not to thrust into her. Hell, it was all I could do not to come all over the sheets. But I had an agenda and it was a damn important one. If I couldn't *show* her how I felt, there was a good chance she'd want to talk about it again.

When I was satisfied that every drop of orgasm had been wrung out of her, I pulled back and grabbed some pillows to position her for the ultimate penetration. There was one moment of panic when I wondered if there were any rubbers left in the nightstand but there were still three just begging to be used. Then I was on my knees between her legs, nudging her slick opening to make sure I had her full attention.

"I choose who I fuck, Faith."

Without giving her a chance to respond, I thrust balls deep and commanded her to keep her eyes open so she could watch me fuck her. I kept telling her to watch, that it was her I wanted to be inside, her I wanted to fuck and damned if it wasn't having the same affect on my control. Every time I thrust deep, her muscles clenched to try to keep me there, convulsing on my length as I pulled back anyway. Despite the fact that I would have been perfectly happy buried deep inside her all night without twitching a muscle.

God, how could she even think I didn't want her?

I told her I did, I showed her I did and now it was her turn. "I want to hear you tell me you want me. You want this."

Yeah, I wanted to hear it from her too. While I was buried deep inside her, one thrust away from satisfying us both.

"I do want you—and this!"

Oh, fuck! I touched her clit as a reward and that was it for her. Her orgasm grabbed me on a deep thrust and held me there, shooting jolts of electricity through my balls and up my spine. I felt her eyes on me, caressing me as waves of heat flowed through my dick and I collapsed on top of her.

Wow, that had been hot. Hot enough to melt vanilla beans.

Chapter Fifteen

Faith does what she came to Vegas to do

While returning to Ivan's, Dorian made a call on his cell, then told me Ivan had found a guy who knew a guy who was supposed to be an even better mind-wiping hypnotist than Larry the lounge lizard. So we needed to return to Ivan's house for more than just sweeping up glass from his walkway.

I needed to know more about the process so asked Dorian what he planned to do—in detail.

"Ivan and I discussed this and I think we've come up with a good plan. The hypnotist will first demonstrate his skill by making us write something on a piece of paper and then wipe our memories of doing it. Afterward, he'll produce the messages we wrote."

"And we'll know what a genius he is." *Yeah, right.* No one could hypnotize me. I had tried it once at a friend's bachelorette party. No way was I going to make out with a rubber chicken. "So when you say 'we' will participate in this little demonstration, you mean me."

"No, I'll do it too."

The fact that Dorian was willing to undergo the experience surprised me. That is, until I remembered his thoroughness. Of course he'd want to go through it. He'd want to see for himself how it worked. Not only that but I could simply pretend to have had my mind wiped, which is exactly what I planned to do.

I couldn't be hypnotized and I knew that. To be extra sure, I'd simply resist. I'd talk over him in my brain and tell myself what a load of hogwash they were trying to feed me. Who knows what the Doms would really try to do while I was under. For all I knew, Dorian, or more likely, Ivan might ask him to turn me into a sweet, well-behaved little submissive simply for their own amusement. *Ha, ha. Look at the vanilla princess go down on every phallic symbol in the room.* Nope. Hypnosis was not for me.

It didn't matter anyway. If we did wind up getting married, I couldn't testify against him in court for having the BDSM club. My conscience would be clear and I'd talk him into selling it at some point after that. Don't doubt my ability to do that. I took lessons from the best guilt tripper that ever lived. My mother.

"He'll also have to plant a false memory or two in our minds," Dorian said.

"Huh? Like what?"

"Like how we met. Why we came to Vegas."

I folded my arms in front of my seat-belted chest. "And what did you and Ivan decide as far as that's concerned?"

"Ivan has no say in it. That part's up to you and me."

I tipped my head and thought about how I would

have liked to meet Dorian on my wedding day. I couldn't erase the memory of leaving Roger at the altar. My mother would know something was wrong and wouldn't stop probing until she either found the truth or drove me out of my friggin' mind. Probably both.

"I'm stumped. How could I have met you on my wedding day?"

"Maybe you didn't. Maybe we met a few days before and you couldn't go through with it after knowing your true love and soul mate wasn't the man at the altar."

He glanced over at me and smiled. I looked for a hint of sarcasm and couldn't find it. I would have said it with sarcasm and then gauged his reaction—had I thought of it. Okay. So I'm still insecure and apt to cover it up with my favorite defense mechanism. That's from Know Thyself 101.

"Do you really think we're soul mates? If so, that means fate put us together and fate must have a twisted sense of humor." If I was going to try this honesty thing, I might as well start now.

He brushed my cheek with the backs of his fingers. The sensation sent shivers through me.

"I don't know if such a thing exists. All I know for sure is that I love you in a whole new way and want to see where this leads."

"By 'whole new way' you mean…"

"I mean that, for once, I can't predict the outcome of every interaction I have with my lady. I don't have to tell you what to do and how to do it every minute of the day. I'm not bored to tears."

No one had ever been able to drive away not only my sarcastic words but my sarcastic thoughts too. For once, I couldn't poke holes in anything he said or did. Seeing this through might be the best or the worst thing ever but we'd never know which if we didn't try. Frankly, I doubted there would be a middle ground.

* * * * *

Ivan couldn't believe I had returned voluntarily. I couldn't believe that Nina was still there, leaning over the sofa, displaying her red-striped butt! And apparently she had cleaned up the glass first. Well, fine. I didn't much like the idea of being treated like a naughty child. But if she was okay with it, good for her.

Dorian handed me the yellow pages. I knew exactly what he wanted me to do and a big part of me wanted to defy him, if only for Nina's sake. I knew I really didn't have a leg to stand on, though. I had broken the glass and someone else had cleaned it up. I guess the least I could do was call a glass shop to replace it.

I flipped through the pages until I came to the word, *Glass,* then asked Dorian, "What's the address so I can send somebody out here?"

He looked surprised. "If you don't already know, it's better that way. Hand me the book."

He took it into the bedroom and closed the door, leaving me with a frowning Dom and a humiliated sub. The tension drove me into the kitchen where I had intended to listen to Dorian's part of the conversation. I had been in too big a hurry to figure out the name of the road, never mind the approximate number since I didn't remember seeing one. But instead, Ivan joined me.

"Would you like something to drink while we wait?"

"No thanks." I hoped a curt answer would drive him away and I'd be able to hear the address when Dorian gave it to the glass guys. No such luck.

"So did you two decide how you met so Fredrico can plant the new memory?"

Well, we hadn't and I didn't even know the hypnotist's name was Fredrico but I really didn't want to carry on a conversation with Ivan so I just said, "No."

Suddenly I heard the water running in the bathroom. So, I guess Dorian must not be in the bedroom, after all. He wouldn't be talking on his cell phone as he used the facilities, would he? No. That would be gross.

"Well, I have an idea," he said. "I think you two could have met—"

"Dorian said he and I would decide that." I'm not usually so impolite but if this guy didn't shut up, I'd never be able to overhear the address. Of course, it might be difficult to hear over the running water too. Had they figured out I had supersonic hearing?

At last, the water shut off and Dorian joined us in the kitchen. "The glass company should be here tomorrow. I called the club and gave them an update too."

I don't know why I should care but I had to ask. "Is everything okay back home?"

He smiled in that way that makes me want to kiss him for no reason. "Yes. Everything's fine."

Ivan raised his eyebrows. "Are you two in love or something?"

I waited for Dorian to speak. The infuriating man was hesitating, waiting for me. So I shrugged. Then he shrugged. We both began laughing at the same time.

"Yeah, I see what's going on," Ivan said. "Well, if you two would like to be alone, I'm going to take Nina home, now. Fredrico won't be here until six thirty."

Dorian and I looked at each other with grateful smiles.

"I knew it," Ivan said. "I put a few more toys in the bedside drawer and a pair of love cuffs—just in case."

Chapter Fifteen and a Half
Dorian's friend, Ivan

I laid out the plan for her as best I could as we headed back to Ivan's house. Since I had my phone back, I was able to call ahead and make sure he and Nina were done and that the hypnotist was either there or on his way.

Faith seemed surprised that I was willing to go through the process with her. It was only fair and I was willing as long as the hypnotist planted something in our minds so that we could meet again. I was willing to let her go only if it meant we got to start all over again.

I didn't tell her but that meant turning over the club to be run by someone else. It was too profitable to walk away completely and hey, it was a family legacy and all that but I didn't need to be part of the day-to-day operations. I also had plenty of other investments I could live off until I figured out what I wanted to do. Besides spend an entire year in bed with Faith.

Despite my call ahead, or maybe because of it, we did get a bit of a show when we arrived at Ivan's house. The glass had been cleaned up but Ivan had positioned Nina bare-ass-up over the couch, her numerous welts showing in all their glory. Neither of them looked unhappy about it. I briefly wondered if Ivan was trying to show me what I'd be missing but he only had eyes for Nina. Faith and I were simply part of her punishment.

Speaking of which, it was as good a time as any for Faith's punishment. I handed her the phone book and she did try to make a call to the glass company for a replacement window but I ended up taking over the call when she asked for Ivan's address. With my luck, it would be the one piece of information she retained and she'd have the local cops investigating him to find out why his address was familiar. I took care of my own business while I was at it. There would be legal documents to sign later but for now, things were in place.

Well, everything except Fredrico. Apparently, he was unavailable until six thirty. I was a bit put out by that until Ivan said he and Nina were leaving and oh, by the way, he'd supplied our room with more toys and a pair of love cuffs to pass the time.

Damn. Friends like that were hard to find. I was going to miss him.

Chapter Sixteen
Fred, the Amazing

Fredrico finally arrived at about eight p.m. I'm glad he gave Dorian and me plenty of time for our fun and games, plus a shower afterward. Whew! I needed a super shower after my crazy reactions to his spicy lovemaking. You know how he said he'd never get bored with me? Well, ditto!

Yeah, so back to Fredrico. I had expected an older man with a beard and turban. I wasn't prepared for the drop-dead-sexy young guy who walked into Ivan's living room. He had long, tousled black hair and wore all black clothing. His intense black eyes glittered as if he could hypnotize an inanimate object with only a look. Maybe he could. *No, no Faith, don't think like that!* I had to keep my skepticism alive and well. I had to sing show tunes in my head if necessary. Anything but concentrate on emptying my mind of anything but his voice. I've seen these guys work before.

Dorian shook his hand and seemed happy to see him. "I'm glad you could make it, man. You're saving my ass, here."

Fredrico—I still didn't know if that was his first or last name—didn't crack a smile.

"This is Faith?" he asked in a Slavic accent as he nodded toward me.

"Yes," I answered. I figured the less said, the better. Maybe I was right because he paused as if waiting to hear more, then just snorted.

"She will be difficult."

Dorian lifted his eyebrows. "How do you know?"

"I just know."

He kept staring at me, so I shifted my gaze to Dorian. "What do you say, lover? Want to get this show on the road?"

"Yeah. We should do this as soon as possible. I think Fredrico has some kind of commitment tonight."

That's when he finally smiled but only briefly. Whatever was going on after this, he probably couldn't wait to get to it. Good. Maybe he'd rush through.

"Sit on the couch," he said.

Dorian and I sat next to each other. He gave my thigh a reassuring squeeze.

"Now the first thing I want to do is have you both write something on a piece of paper." He eyed me suspiciously. "In your usual handwriting, write something you can prove. Something you will have no doubt you wrote only minutes before. Then I will erase that one thing from your minds."

Ivan handed us both a notebook and pencil. I was tempted to be a smart-ass and write down the address of the club but since that was the one thing they wanted me to forget I didn't think it would be appreciated. Besides, I'd be blocking my mind so I'd remember it anyway.

I tapped my lips with the eraser and tried to think of something no one but me would know. I wasn't about to use the nickname Roger gave me. Not after it made the Sergeant laugh so hard. *Think, Faith. Think.*

Dorian had already scribbled something and handed the notebook to Fredrico. All eyes were on me, now.

"I'm thinking. I'm thinking!"

"It's no big deal, Faith." Dorian said. "Just write down the first thing that comes to mind."

Okay, I had something. I turned so no one could see what I wrote and in my best cursive writing, I penned, "Red, furry love cuffs are in the guest room and I'd like to see Ivan wearing them with Nina flogging his ass. Oh—and the flogger is under the bed."

Before anyone could see what I had written, I handed the notebook to Fredrico. He glanced at it and smiled, slightly. "Are you sure this is what you want everyone to hear after I awaken you?"

"Most definitely," I said and crossed my arms.

Fredrico shrugged and set the notebooks aside. "Now get as comfortable as you can. Take your shoes off if you like. Lie down if you want to."

I angled my body so I could rest my head on Dorian's lap and stretch out on the couch. "Is this comfortable for you, lover?" Maybe this way he'd remember that we were close, even if the demon hypnotist tried to erase it from his mind.

He stroked my hair and gazed down at me. "Perfectly," he said.

Fredrico focused on my eyes. "All right. I want you to tune out everything but my voice. Listen only to the sound of my voice and relax."

Show tune time! *Ohhhhhklahoma with the wind whip, whipping…* Oh no, that's not a good one. Let's see…

Fredrico was saying we needed to close our eyes and that sounded like a good idea, anyway. His eyes made me squeamish. I closed my eyes and tried to think of a song I actually knew the words to. *You are my sunshine, my only sunshine…* Nope that wouldn't do, either.

"Dorian. Are you completely relaxed?" he asked.

"Yes," Dorian responded sounding kind of far away.

Oh yeah. He was under. I had to sing something in my mind as soon as he'd asked me the same question.

"Faith? Are you completely relaxed?"

"Yes," I said, trying to imitate Dorian's voice.

"Good. I want you to relax even more. Go deeper and deeper into relaxation…"

Super-cali-fragilistic-expialido-cious, even though the sound of it…

I felt Dorian go limp beneath me. Well, all of him except the one large bump under my head. Good to know I could turn him on even under hypnosis. I guess his attraction to me couldn't be erased.

Fredrico asked Dorian to repeat what he had written backward. He did but the message was hard to decipher. I had heard my name, so I tried to figure it out but then it occurred to me that if he asked me to repeat what I wrote backward, I might not be able to do it. Damn.

Think, Faith. What did you write?

Fortunately, he was still talking to Dorian. I heard

the word, *Forget*, a few times, so I had to go back to my movie soundtrack and hope for the best.

Hmm hmm hmm hmm you'll always seem precocious. Super-cali-fragilistic-expialido-cious!

Happily, he didn't ask me to repeat my phrase backward. He was simply telling me to forget all about the toys in the guest room. Forget the red love cuffs in there and forget that a flogger was stashed under the bed.

I could easily pretend to forget those things. No one would see how wet I got just thinking about what we did. *Oops.* I almost giggled out loud. Better begin singing another—

"Wake up!" Fredrico shouted.

Bolting upright, I gasped. "Jeez, Louise! You don't need to yell."

Dorian's eyes fluttered open, then he stretched and yawned. "Wow, I feel like I've had a really refreshing nap."

Fredrico nodded, sagely. "That's because I suggested you'd feel that way. Faith?"

"Huh? Oh yeah. Me too. Feel all refreshed and ready for anything."

"I was going to ask you if you remember what you wrote."

"Oh. Well, nothing. I don't remember a thing."

"And Dorian? Do you remember?"

"No. Nothing."

Fredrico handed us the notebooks and there was my message, written in my own hand. Now I had to act surprised. I glanced over at Dorian and he smiled at his notebook.

"What does yours say?"

"It says you have a birthmark in the shape of an

apple on your ass."

"I do not!"

He shrugged. "I guess we'll find out."

If I did, I sure didn't know about it. Had I ever looked at my own ass? Naked? Now that I thought about it, I probably hadn't. I only checked out that part of my anatomy when checking for panty-lines in Bloomingdale's three-way mirror. And I tried never to check it out in my uniform. Those baggy pants did nobody's butt justice.

"I suggest you two go to the guest room and check your new information. If you find that what you wrote is true, it will prove my ability to remove an item from your memory."

* * * * *

"Well, I'll be damned." I glanced in the small mirror Dorian held behind my right butt cheek so I could see the apple-shaped birthmark. "How weird is that?"

"It's only weird that we're both discovering it for the first time. I think it's cute."

As I kneeled on the bed, he ran his hand over my bare ass and I tingled. *Don't get distracted, now, Faith. It's almost over.* "Awww... It's nice of you to lie."

"Are you telling me I'm not being honest with you? I'm always honest with you, Faith."

"No. I, uh…"

He patted my butt and set the mirror down. "Remember when you said, if you love every inch of a person, you can overlook all kinds of things?"

"I guess so. It sounds like something I'd say." I sat on the butt cheek in question.

"I told you that I love you." He sat beside me. "Why would I be upset about a tiny apple birthmark?"

"I don't know. Just don't call me apple-butt, okay?"

He grinned and kissed my cheek—the one that was beginning to blush. "Only if you won't call me names, either."

"Okay, so no hitting and no name calling. How am I supposed to blow off steam if I get super pissed at you?"

"Just talk to me. You'd be surprised how easy it is to work things out with a simple, civil conversation."

"Is that what you tell your subs?"

He raised his eyebrows. "I don't have subs anymore. But when I did…yes. Why wouldn't I?"

I shrugged, then leaned over and pulled the flogger out from under the bed. "Oh, I don't know. I figured Doms just let these things communicate for them."

A frown passed over his face like a dark, storm cloud. "Only if talking doesn't work. Didn't you listen to anything I told you? Doms want their subs' happiness as much as subs want to make their Doms happy."

"I want you to be happy but I'm not a sub."

"That's what love is all about, sweetheart—each person does what they can to please the other, or others—and how did that thing get under there?"

"I put it there. I mean when Ivan said he put toys in our room, I saw this before you came in and hid it. I had no intention of letting you use it on me."

"And you remember hiding it there—even after the hypnosis?"

"Well, no. Not really. I mean, I remember seeing it but I forgot where I hid it until I read the notebook where I wrote that it was under the bed."

"Oh." He looked at me askance but didn't pursue it any further.

Whew.

"Fredrico is expecting us back any minute, so you might want to put your skirt on—although I hate saying goodbye to your beautiful birthmark."

"Oh, yeah?" I decided to be a little *cheeky* and bent over at the waist to pick up my panties from where they'd landed. He slapped my butt and I flinched.

"Hey!"

"Sorry. I couldn't resist. You have the cutest ass."

"Sweet talker."

Chapter Sixteen and a Half
Dorian becomes suspicious

Fredrico was late but anyone who gave me a whole hour and a half with Faith, love cuffs and a whole array of dildos was okay in my book. Kudos to Ivan too, for providing all the toys and leaving any pain implements out of the picture. I would have hated to have to kill him for killing the mood.

When the hypnotist finally did arrive, I was sated and one hundred percent sure we were doing the right thing. I don't think Faith was so sure but she was definitely game.

The test part was easy. I wrote down Faith's adorable birthmark but she wasn't writing anything. Gee and here I thought I'd impressed her with my big nine-inch— She'd started writing before I had to lean down and remind her. It would have sounded like bragging and any guy with a big dick knew that guys who felt the need to brag about it were lying.

It didn't help that I could tell Faith had thought Fredrico was hot when she saw him. Maybe I didn't like him so much after all. We were trusting him with an awful lot.

Then Faith stretched out and laid her head in my lap and I wished the hypnotist would go away for another hour and a half. I stroked her soft hair and tried to relax, tried to ignore the way the back of her head pressed against my boner.

Next thing I knew, Fredrico was yelling at me to wake up. What the fuck? There was no need to yell. I must have just dozed off for a moment. I felt great! Oh, right. He'd said to relax. That's when it hit me that this hypnotism shit really worked!

I couldn't wait to prove it, especially when Faith denied her birthmark existed. I wasn't stupid. The only way to prove that was to have her strip and bend over for me. Damn, I really wish she had written down my dick size. Only one way to prove that too.

That's when Faith went and pulled a flogger out from under the bed. It was only a small one that didn't even sport a single knot in the leather strands but I changed my mind about killing Ivan for providing it. Better yet, I felt like going to get him so he could have the ensuing *talk* with Faith.

Once again, I had to convince her that I wasn't interested in her being a typical sub. I say typical because whether she was a natural one or not was still up in the air. It didn't matter. I just wanted her to be Faith and everything that entailed, including her cop uniform and yeah, her mother. I don't mean to sound callous because I did understand where the insecurity was coming from. All I had to do was put myself in her shoes if she was the Dom and I was vanilla. I'd be wondering what the fuck she was doing with me too.

Something was bugging me about the whole

flogger thing, though, and it had nothing to do with Dom and sub. It wasn't until we were in front of Fredrico again that I realized what it was. Faith had said she remembered actually *putting* the flogger under the bed but that memory should have been erased. She should have found out where it was but only because it was written in her notebook.

Chapter Seventeen
Suspicion averted. Moving on

"So Fredrico," Dorian asked, "If something triggers a memory, will whatever you erased come back?"

Fredrico shook his head. "It shouldn't. Whatever the person is experiencing at the time might feel like déjà vu but that's all. Nothing specific will return."

"So if you only erase part of a memory, the part you didn't erase may return?"

"What are you asking?"

Dorian looked at me. "What did you erase from Faith's mind?"

"Only what she told me from the notebook. The location of the items she mentioned and her desire to see them used on a particular person."

His eyebrows shot up.

"Oh, not you, lover," I interjected.

"Okay…"

"Why? What's wrong?" Fredrico asked.

"She said she remembered *putting* the flogger under

the bed."

"No, I didn't!" I may have said that a little too forcefully. "I realized I must have put it there because I remembered seeing it and wanting to hide it. I totally forgot where it was though." I appealed to Fredrico's egotism. "Seriously, you were friggin' amazing. I was so surprised to find it there. Unreal!"

He beamed. "Of course."

"So," Dorian continued in his annoyingly thorough way, "we must be specific and complete about what needs to be erased from her mind."

"Yes," Fredrico said. "Do you need more time to consider all the particulars? I could come back tomorrow."

Ivan walked in and voiced his opinion. "No. I think we'd better do this now but make sure they write down everything and review it together, so nothing is missed."

Fredrico nodded. "That would be wise." He handed Dorian a notebook. "Be as specific as you can."

I looked at him and said, "I don't want you to forget what we mean to each other." Then I winked. "And I'd like to remember *most* things we've done together."

He smiled. "Same here."

"So how do we deal with little details like why I was always tied up and trying to escape?"

"Exactly." He looked to Fredrico, pencil poised in the air.

Fredrico shrugged one shoulder and looking smug, he said, "Piece of cake. I can make you remember it as role-playing, or I can eliminate the memory of bonds and the desire to escape altogether."

Dorian nodded. "Okay, that sounds good. She needs to forget about being kidnapped too. And we mostly need for her to forget about the existence of my club."

"Absolutely. Give me all the particulars. The name and address of the club, what you do there, everything you want her to forget. Meanwhile, you should give me another story to fill in the blanks. She'll surely have questions about what she doesn't know and why. Ivan, do you have anything to occupy my time so they don't feel rushed?"

"I have a pool table downstairs. Do you play?"

"Not well but it might be good to practice."

Oh great. Now I have to listen to balls banging into each other.

"How about taking a couple of beers down with us?"

"Fine."

As soon as they headed toward the kitchen, Dorian wrote down the name of the club and the address, then "owner and participant" next to that.

"Participant?"

"Don't you want to forget that I engaged in the whole lifestyle?"

I thought it best to play along. "Yeah, I guess so. What are you going to tell me you do instead?"

"We can keep lying to a minimum if we just say I'm a businessman and Fredrico can give you the address and phone number of my other office."

"Shouldn't I know what kind of business you're in? After all, I ran away to Vegas with you. We must have talked. That probably would have come up." Hey, I wanted to sound convincing and I was curious about what he'd say.

Dorian shrugged. "Say I'm in finance. I like making money."

"So you're a stockbroker or something?"

He shook his head. "No..." After a thoughtful moment, he said, "Call me an investor. I make money from other people's ideas."

"That sounds plausible but where did you get the capital to invest?"

"I inherited it. That much is true."

I pointed to the notebook. "That all sounds good. Write it down."

He frowned at me as if to say, *don't tell me what to do, woman,* but eventually he shook his head and did it anyway. I needed to remember that this would be an adjustment for both of us—at least until my memory was "erased"—then I could go back to being my usual, no-nonsense self and he couldn't say much about it without revealing his past. Heh heh.

"So," he said, "how do you think we should have met?"

I began to sing, "I met him at the candy stoooooore...Dorian started to laugh, then coughed to cover it.

"What? Some of the cops got together and formed a fifties band. They were pretty good too."

"I'm betting you weren't in it, though."

"Are you saying I can't sing?"

He put his arm around me and whispered, "Let me put it this way. Your mouth has other talents."

Wow, I didn't realize I was so tone-deaf. No wonder animals howl when I sing. I thought they were singing along. But I couldn't get mad. At least the insult came with a terrific compliment.

"How about the candy aisle in a grocery store?" he

asked. "Where do you shop?"

"Little Giant Mart."

He cocked his head. "Is this just you being silly or do you really shop at a store called 'Little Giant Mart'?"

I stuck my hand on my hip and faked annoyance. "I'm not the only clever person in the world, you know."

"Oh, clever. That's what we're calling it these days?"

I reached for the pillow, ready to bop him with it but remembered how he wanted me to act and just huffed instead.

"Fine, sometimes I go to the local farmers' market."

"They don't have candy, do they?"

"No but they have natural honey. I buy that once in a while."

"How old is your latest jar of honey?"

I tipped my head and tried to remember. "Well, the expiration date probably went by two or three years ago."

He rolled his eyes. "That won't work. You'll wonder where the honey is when you get home."

"Hey, that happens sometimes. You know how you'd swear on your life that you bought toothpaste but when you get home...no toothpaste? Maybe people get temporarily hypnotized in the grocery store. Shopping is boring enough to put anyone in a stupor."

He gave me "the pause". You know what I'm talking about? When the person you're conversing with just looks at you but doesn't respond and you know they're not going to react—ever. You could sit there until the next morning, waiting for a response and they'd still be staring at you like you had two heads.

Finally, he broke the silence. "What candy have you bought recently, or for that matter, any consumable you buy every week?"

Was there anything I bought every week? I didn't want to say I met him in the toilet paper aisle. That wouldn't be sexy. "Look, how about if we just bumped into each other at the coffee shop? Maybe you spilled your extra grande, decaf, mocha latte on me?"

"Got anything in your laundry basket with a coffee stain?"

I threw my hands in the air. "Okay, then you come up with something!"

"Fine. We met at Little Giant Mart in front of the candy display. I asked if you could recommend a candy as sweet as you."

"And I inwardly groaned over your terrible line but you were cute, so I said, 'Yeah—those hot cinnamon things'."

"And I said, 'I love spice'. That would do it." He wrote all of that down too. If I didn't laugh during this fake mental reenactment, Fredrico would.

"Okay, so what did we do after the grocery store?" I asked.

"I asked you out for coffee."

"I would have said, *no*. Engaged...remember?"

"Do you?"

What kind of dumb question was that? Of course, I remembered. "What kind of girl do you think I am?"

"One who had second thoughts? Maybe one who

had to explore why she responded so viscerally to a total stranger even though she was supposed to be in love? Maybe one who suddenly realized that she didn't have to settle for someone she wasn't in love with? Maybe one who believes in love at first sight now that it's happened to both of us?"

"Is that last part true? I mean, for you?"

He grinned. "Yes it is."

"I-I…" I had no comeback. "Yeah, okay. That'll do."

As we hammered out all the details of our so-called *normal* whirlwind relationship, everything made sense. Even the part about the whirlwind.

"Faith?"

"Yeah?"

"Will you marry me? For real?"

I gasped. My eyes watered. For once in my life I was rendered utterly speechless. My thoughts whirled. If I didn't return to New Jersey with a wedding ring on my finger, my mother would badger me for the rest of my life—or until I caved and married Roger in a small private ceremony. That would be my intended punishment for inconveniencing everyone the first time—at least in her mind. And just in case the memory of Dorian's club came back to me at some point, a wife didn't have to testify against her husband in a court of law. So marriage was convenient for both of us. But would it be happening if it wasn't necessary?

I couldn't imagine any man willing to go through with a marriage just to keep his club, protect his customers and stay out of jail. Well, okay. I admit that's pretty strong motivation but Fredrico could erase my mind of everything, Dorian included. I couldn't handle that.

I could wander around Las Vegas with amnesia until, somehow, my mother found me—oh, yes, she'd find me all right, with her radar set to "unmarried daughter".

Yes, I loved him like crazy and yes, I'd marry him in a heartbeat but there was something I needed to know first. "Dorian, can I ask you something?"

He stopped scribbling in the notebook and set it down. Facing me, he held my hand, probably sensing the import in my voice. "Of course, love. What is it?"

"Would you be marrying me if I didn't have a badge and a very determined Jewish mother?"

Abruptly, he straightened. "What do you mean?"

"I mean, we're going to say we're in Vegas because we ran away to get married…and we're actually going to go through with it—if I say, 'yes'. If there were another option that didn't include marrying me, would you take it?"

Appearing puzzled, he asked, "Like what?"

"Like erasing my memory of everything, you included."

"Of course not! I love you, Faith. Are you thinking I'm only marrying you to stay out of jail?"

"Maybe."

"I wouldn't do that." He wrapped his free arm around my shoulder and squeezed.

I settled into his sideways embrace and sighed.

"If I married someone I didn't want to be with, I'd eventually lose everything I'd worked for anyway—in a divorce. I don't get backed into corners, Faith. I don't do anything I don't want to do."

"Well, I guess that's true. You didn't want to kill me and here I am."

"Then what's bothering you?"

"I don't know. Would we be doing this if we met under normal circumstances?"

"Are you having second thoughts about marrying me?"

"No."

"It sounds like you are."

"No, Dorian. See if you can understand this. I know what's in my mind and heart but I can't know what's going on in yours. I can hardly believe how much I love you—look at the things I've let you get away with and forgiven you for."

He cracked a smile but didn't say anything.

"I went to someone else's wedding where the bride and groom had known each other for years, were crazy in love and the whole sermon was about how love and marriage require endless forgiveness."

Dorian squinted as if trying to understand an alien. "What does this have to do with me? You just said you forgave me for everything."

I was trying not to get frustrated or say something stupid but eventually I just had to blurt it out. "How do I know you'll always forgive me? I don't know if you've noticed but I can be a bit of a bitch."

He laughed, then he kissed me senseless. When he released me, he said, "I get it. You're worried that I won't be able to forgive you for giving me crap—even though most of it is well deserved."

I nodded, then drew circles on the back of his hand. "I can hardly believe I've finally found someone I can love with all my heart. I'm not settling." Looking into his eyes, trying to see all the way into his soul, I asked, "But are you? You could break my heart. Or let's say this mind wipe works but Fredrico suggests that we're only friends thinking he's helping you to distance yourself even more from a bad situation."

"He won't. I don't want that, either. I'll be nearby and will listen to every word he tells you. I'll stop him if he pulls any funny stuff."

"Promise?"

"I promise." I heard his words not only in his low, velvet voice but also in his amber eyes. Okay, I could do this but I'd still try to resist Fredrico's hypnosis. I trusted Dorian but not Fred.

Instead, I'd concentrate on my handsome, surprising, special honey and how lucky I was. No, how lucky *we* were. He was right. I'm not usually a bitch. And now that there was no more tension between us, we could finally enjoy each other, fully.

"Dorian?"

"Now what?"

"Yes."

Chapter Seventeen and a Half
Dorian Proposes

So the hypnotism was a go. Ivan brought Fredrico downstairs to shoot some pool so Faith and I could hammer out what information we wanted removed and planted for our future. Either Fredrico knew about Ivan's BDSM lifestyle too, or the door to the playroom was closed. I had a feeling it was the former and that's how Ivan had found him. Then again, we were in Vegas. He could have just flipped open the Yellow Pages and looked up BDSM Hypnotist.

Faith and I started the daunting task of creating a believable sound byte for our past. That's when she became a pain in the ass. Then she sang and I learned very quickly that I preferred her to be a pain in the ass.

"Are you saying I can't sing?" she actually had the nerve to ask. Could she not hear herself? Lord knew she certainly heard everything else going on around her.

One hundred and eighty-five pounds of pure

testosterone idiot put his arm around her and answered. "Let me put it this way. Your mouth has other talents."

My body didn't explode in pain. Once again, when she should have hit me, she was smiling like I'd handed her a huge compliment. I had, but I had a feeling if I followed that up by saying, *You give good head, baby*, my balls would reside somewhere near my kidneys.

God, I hoped that part of her wouldn't be changed under hypnosis.

As long as my balls were still exterior, we had work to do. We plodded along and it actually wasn't as hard as you would think until we hit on the fact that she'd been engaged to someone else. Engaged. As in, wanted to marry some Bozo she *didn't love*. Right?

I needed the words. Go figure. Unlike her, though, I could put the words in her mouth and be happy when she agreed that was what she felt. Period. Move on. Why women couldn't do this with all things emotional was beyond me.

But when I opened my mouth, something completely different came out.

"Faith?"

"Yeah?"

"Will you marry me? For real?"

As soon as the words came out of my mouth, I realized I had braced myself. I was half sure she was going to hit me because it was kind of a compliment. She didn't hit me. In fact, she didn't say or do anything except look at me in complete fear for the first time. She might as well have hit me.

When I couldn't take her silence for another second, I went back to writing our ideas in my notebook. Jesus, what the hell had I been thinking? I'd ruined her wedding day, kidnapped her, drugged her and was about to erase her memory. None of that had scared her. She'd been ready to marry someone else so the idea of marriage didn't scare her. The idea of marrying *me*, however…

"Dorian, can I ask you something?"

Shit. She hadn't been in love with the guy, right? She had been settling and now she didn't have to. *Right?*

Okay. If she was suddenly going to tell me she loved the guy she'd left hanging under the *chuppah*, she was going to have to look me in the eye to do it. I put down my notepad and turned to her, taking both her hands in mine. "Of course, love. What is it?"

Her answer stunned me. It was the complete opposite of my fears. She was afraid, yes, afraid I was willing to marry her for the wrong reasons!

I wanted to laugh but at the same time I had a lump in my throat I hadn't felt since my family had died. I managed to swallow it and I was glad I did because I wanted to *talk* to Faith, to tell her how much I loved her and how much her love meant to me. I listened to her words telling me the same thing and I was happier than I'd ever been in my life.

And I didn't even get a boner.

Okay, that last one was a lie.

Chapter Eighteen
Faith won't let go

"Close your eyes and relax. Calm your thoughts as your body relaxes. Push everything away but the sound of my voice. You are becoming more and more relaxed."

And you are becoming more and more annoying, Fred.

"Do you hear anything but the sound of my voice?"

He followed that by dropping a coin on the hard marble floor but having anticipated something like that, I didn't flinch—even though it sounded like a clang to my sensitive audio abilities. I simply said "no," in my most hypnotized-sounding voice.

"Good. I am here to help you forget and remember. Forget unhelpful memories and remember new, recent, happy memories. Do you understand?"

I almost forgot to respond since I went to my own happy place—Dorian's bedroom. Even with one cuff on my wrist, his was the best lovemaking I'd ever experienced and it seemed to only get better and better. I didn't want to forget that. No way. But the object of my adoration sat facing the opposite way, listening to every word spoken. When I eventually answered, "yes," I heard the soft rustle of paper.

"You will forget a club exists at 123 Mason Street in Waterloo, New Jersey. All you know is that a warehouse exists next to an alley and across the street from the Waterloo Police Station. Now, what exists across the street from the police station in which you work?"

"Some warehouse."

"Good. Very good."

He all but patted me on the head before continuing to read from his script.

"You know very little about the lifestyle referred to as *BDSM*. If anyone mentioned it, you might be curious but you wouldn't ask questions since it's not a subject you care to know any more about."

I figured I'd answer with silence unless asked a question by Freddy the Great. As you can surmise, I did my best to remain skeptical of his all-powerful talent with my sarcastic genius. I even got in a few silent Nyaa nyaaas.

"Now, you met your lover, Dorian, in the candy aisle of Little Giant Mart. It was love at first sight. He asked you if you could recommend a candy as sweet as you, to which you responded in your typical flip way, 'Yes. Try those hot, cinnamon things'. Then he gave you his phone number. Isn't that right?"

"Yes," I said, even though he got it slightly wrong.

"You met each other the day before you were supposed to be married to someone else. The instant attraction to Dorian and his to you made you realize that you weren't meant to be with anyone else. That going through with the wedding to Roger would be a mistake, though you tried to anyway. Before it was too late, you ran from the church."

Uh-oh. Was this a trick? Did he just screw up accidentally and say church instead of synagogue or was he trying to convert me to Christianity?

Before I could decide what it would be best to do, I heard the paper rustle and he said, "Ah, yes. Forget I said the word, 'church'. You ran from Temple Beth El."

Whew. Temple, synagogue, either one of those would do. I tried to imagine my mother adjusting not only to a goy son-in-law but two goyim in the family! But, fortunately, I was still in charge of my brain and Dorian was looking out for me so I wouldn't have to start hanging crosses all over my apartment.

Or maybe we'd be living at Dorian's house? We hadn't decided that yet. Oh well, there was time to talk about it later. I'd vote for the cool jewel on the hill over my crappy apartment any day.

"So after you ran, you phoned Dorian. Isn't that correct?"

"Yes," I said. I don't know where I'd have kept Dorian's phone number or the card to make the call but let's just say I not only remembered his number but I remembered my credit card number as well. It could happen—to someone else.

I heard him sigh with relief. "Good. Very good."

This time I think he was patting himself on the head.

"Dorian met you at the coffee shop you frequent and drove you to his home. Is that right?"

"Yes."

"You were too enamored of him and too conflicted internally to remember how you got there but you remember his home."

Another pause. This time he turned the page first, then finished his thought. "You two talked much of the night, realized you were deeply in love and wanted to spend the rest of your lives together. You remember this, don't you?"

"Yes. I remember." I wanted to remember. I wished our journey had begun that way as unlikely as that version was. Of course, what really happened was pretty unlikely as well but the candy aisle would make a better story for our grandchildren. Would we have grandchildren? Ha! If my mother has anything to say about it...

"Then you made love, sealing your fates. Mating with the one person in the entire world made just for you. Your love has grown with every minute you've spent together and you won't let anyone or anything ruin the love you share. It's the most powerful emotion you've ever had. It's too precious to jeopardize in any way. Isn't that right?"

I felt a tear forming in the corner of my eye and hoped it didn't roll down my cheek. Who knew if that would tip him off? The last words he spoke were true, so true they touched something deep in my heart.

"Yes," I said with a shaky voice.

"Good," he cooed. "Very, very good. When you awaken in a few moments, you will be looking forward to your real wedding. The one you and Dorian came to Las Vegas for. You will only know me as a shaman who came to bless and enhance your union. Do you understand?"

I couldn't even speak. I could only nod but

apparently that was enough.

"One, two, three. Wake up!" He snapped his fingers in front of my face and I jumped.

"Wha… Oh dear, I must have fallen asleep! How rude of me," I said, hoping he was convinced I'd been under the whole time.

He smiled. It was a gentle, sweet smile this time. "It's all right. I seem to have that affect on people."

Dorian stretched and yawned then wrapped me in his arms as if I were the most precious treasure on the earth. "I love you so much," he whispered.

"Well, you're tired. I must go now," Fredrico said. "I just wanted to congratulate you both."

"You'll come to the wedding, won't you?" I asked. That might have been a little over the top but I wanted to play this out so there'd be no question about my cooperation.

"I would be honored. When will it be?"

Dorian and I looked at each other. We hadn't talked about that.

"The sooner the better," he said, then tipped my face up and kissed me so tenderly I thought I might slide out of his arms and onto the floor, like a cartoon character.

"We'll call you," I said. Whether we did or not really didn't matter to me. I simply wanted Fredrico to leave so Dorian and I could be alone, together.

Chapter Eighteen and a Half
Dorian goes under

"Close your eyes and relax," Fredrico's smooth voice ordered Faith. "Calm your thoughts as your body relaxes."

Good girl. She was going through with it. I was not only in the room, I had my back up against Faith's and I could feel her tension ebbing as she followed the hypnotist's orders. I knew not to face the guy but I wasn't going to be happy unless I knew he had followed our instructions to the letter.

Fredrico was doing fine. The tone of those orders was so smooth, so melodic. "Push everything away but the sound of my voice. You are becoming more and more relaxed…"

The next thing I heard was someone snapping their fingers and I realized Faith must have fallen asleep because the shaman was trying to wake her up. Damn, I could only hope he didn't realize I'd fallen asleep too. All that sex must have worn us out.

I got a funny picture in my head of having to tie

Faith to the bed after a couple of rounds so we could get a little sleep to regenerate. No sooner had the thought crossed my mind than I was hit with a boner the size of the Stratosphere. Huh. Obviously getting some sleep was key.

The shaman—what the hell was his name?—gave me what looked strangely like a go-ahead nod. I stretched and yawned to give myself a minute. It didn't help. I stood and wrapped my arms around Faith, nudging her to let her in on my embarrassing problem.

That's when I stopped giving a crap if the shaman noticed. Had Ivan really thought a shaman's blessing was necessary? For the life of me, I couldn't remember Ivan being into that kind of stuff. Actually, I couldn't think of a whole heck of a lot I did know about Ivan, other than the fact that this was his house and he wasn't in the room.

If the shaman had a problem with my having a hard-on for my fiancée, he would just have to deal with it. I had my sweet Faith in my arms.

"I love you so much," I whispered in her ear and then nudged her again.

She must have thought I had a kosher dill in my pocket because she was taking the time to invite the guy to our wedding. And crap, we hadn't set a date or time.

I mumbled something about the sooner the better and kissed my bride to be in a way that left no doubt we wanted to be alone. The shaman finally got the message and left, no doubt to eat some magical herb so he could get lucky too.

I could have told him it was useless. There was only one Faith and she was mine. It was time to show her how much I appreciated that fact with some nice, slow lovemaking.

Chapter Nineteen
Sealing it with a kiss and then some

Fully dressed, rolling around on the bed and making out, Dorian said, "That was nice of that shaman to stop by just to bless our future," then he French-kissed me, for about the dozenth time.

My cop antenna vibrated over my head. Dorian wasn't acting like himself. And he had been listening in on the hypno-session. Hmmm… *Listening in.* Was that enough for him to go under?

I suddenly remembered the hypnosis tape I'd bought for relaxation ages ago when I first started the job. That hypnotist hadn't been in the room with me. All I had to do was listen to her voice. I realized that Dorian just might have succumbed whereas I resisted and didn't. What was it Fredrico said? If you trusted the hypnotist, anyone could be hypnotized? And wasn't it Dorian who believed in all this shit in the first place? Didn't the guy prove his power to Dorian's satisfaction? *Bada Bing!*

I could hardly believe my luck. If Dorian had

swallowed everything—every suggestion—then he wouldn't know about the club's existence. *Holy kreplach.* He'd barely know anything about BDSM and wouldn't even be curious about it! As far as he knew he was a businessman investor. A vanilla one, at that!

I wanted to dance for joy. Whatever sex we'd have in the future would probably be just as fantastic as before since Fred didn't try to rub out *that* information, thank God—just the BDSM stuff.

Now, what kind of test could prove if his mind was really wiped or not? I racked my brain as Dorian continued to kiss and nibble like I was made of candy. Ah! The candy!

I said something about how I felt…what was it? Something about even though it was a cheesy line, he was cute so I went along. The hypnotist said other stuff that he wouldn't have known unless I told him—which I hadn't. "Dorian?" I asked when he finally came up for air.

"Yes, my love?"

"Remember when we met?"

"I'll never forget it." He swirled his tongue in my ear and I shivered.

"Do you remember what you said when you first spoke to me?"

He paused and peered into my eyes. "Of course. I asked if you could recommend a candy as sweet as you. I know you thought it was a cheesy line."

"Hmmm… How did you know that?"

He shrugged. "I don't know. I just did—I guess."

"Oh. By the way, did that shaman say anything about me running from a church?"

"No. I don't remember him saying anything like that. In fact, I don't remember much of what he said.

I'm afraid I dozed off."

Bingo!

* * * * *

"Lie flat on your back."

Dorian looked surprised at first, then did as I asked.

"Move your butt all the way to the edge of the bed." I added a sly smile so as not to sound just plain bossy. I want to suck you hard, then ride you backward."

He grinned and scooted down as if playing *Simon says*, only he didn't ask, "May I?" I didn't need to go that far to see if his reprogramming extended to sex.

I rolled off the bed and walked around to where he was splayed like a woman about to get her annual pelvic exam. I'd have laughed except I really didn't want to humiliate him. I just wanted to see if he could give up control—for once.

I bent over him, unbuttoned and unzipped his fly, then yanked his legs out and stripped the pants off.

"Wow," he said. "You don't fool around when you're horny, do you?"

"Should I?" I asked. "Would you rather I hint? Beat around the bush, knowing maybe you'd get it and maybe you wouldn't?"

"Are you kidding? What man wouldn't want to be stripped naked by a gorgeous woman and fucked?"

So far, so good. "I hoped you'd feel that way."

He pulled his black boxers off his legs so fast that the smile on his face went with them. He began to sit up. I shoved him back down, fisted his erection and pumped.

Dorian closed his eyes and groaned.

"Do you like that, lover?" I asked.

"Yeah," he said, "but…" and his breath hitched.

"Do you want me to go down on you with my mouth?"

"Later. I want to go down on you, first."

What red-blooded American girl could turn that down? Not me. Besides, I had my answer. He was an ingrained Alpha male and just had to steer the ship.

He stood, turned me around and pushed on my shoulders so I was the one sitting on the end of the bed. I swallowed hard as he undressed me, his eyes smoking with lust. His erection brushed my leg and I squirmed at the thought of that gorgeous cock sliding into my center, now damp and heated.

I could see in his liquid-looking eyes that he wanted to fuck me. But as desperately as he wanted that, he was also willing to postpone his own pleasure to make sure I was primed and ready for him.

He kneeled on the floor and I parted my legs until I was completely exposed to him. An aching throb invaded my pussy and I couldn't wait until he slaked the craving, replacing the emptiness with his full length.

He rested his hands on my thighs and leaned in to lick my wet folds. I gasped and arched up to him, spreading my legs impossibly wider.

He capitalized on the improved access and speared my opening with his tongue. As he lapped away the juices, I hoped he wasn't trying to prevent them from running onto the bedspread. I figured it was a lost cause. We'd simply have to toss the thing in the washing machine later.

He sucked my clit and I nearly lost it. Then he flicked away with his tongue. One second, two seconds and on the third second of titillating my clit, my orgasm struck—hard. I arched my back and slammed against the bed as he relentlessly raked his tongue back and forth over my pulsing clitoris. I quivered and cried out over and over like an ambulance siren as I kept coming and coming. Eventually, I quieted and savored the aftershocks.

Dorian came up for air. He stood over me, his raging hard-on a contradiction to the satisfied look on his face. He must have known I was boneless. He leaned over and sucked on one tightly beaded nipple. All I could do was writhe and moan.

"No more," I managed to croak, breathlessly.

"Then how am I supposed to take care of this?" he asked, gesturing to his swollen cock.

I scooted backward on the bed as fast as my shaky legs would let me, let my knees fall open and said, "Go for it."

"Are you sure?"

My hollow cavern reminded me just how empty it was by clenching involuntarily. "Please. I want you."

He grabbed a condom, crawled up next to me and straightened out the knee closest to him. Then he lay on his side and pulled me up on my side, facing him. "Put your leg over me."

"The one you turned to jelly?"

He smiled and grabbed my ankle sliding my leg over his hip. Prodding my pussy lips with the head of his cock, he said, "We're going to fuck lying on our sides."

"Whatever you want," was all I could manage to say. I couldn't have fought him off even if it wasn't fine by me but fortunately, I wanted him inside me, gliding in and out of me as badly as he wanted to fuck. He found my opening with his fingers first, then steered his erection in. We both sighed with relief. This position didn't allow the deep penetration that others did but I was happy to be hugging him in a couple of different ways and he seemed content with it too.

He nuzzled my neck as he began to move. Ah, heaven. I found a little leftover energy—just enough—and met his thrusts with my pelvis. His breathing deepened and he increased his pace, panting.

A few minutes of delicious fucking and he stiffened. He jerked several times and grunted. I was glad he came. I wanted him to feel as satisfied as I did. I didn't need to come again. I just loved the feel of him inside me and my hunger was completely slaked.

Chapter Nineteen and a Half
Dorian's reward

We were back in our guest room, making out like teenagers, when I got my first clue that she was thinking more along the lines of fast and furious.

"Lie flat on your back," she demanded after a particularly hot tongue duel.

I did what she said. We weren't even married yet and I knew not to ignore that tone of voice.

I was rewarded when she demanded more. "Move your butt all the way to the edge of the bed. I want to suck you hard, then ride you backward."

See? I wasn't an idiot. It had a weird, unnatural feel to it but I didn't stop her until she had my dick in her hand, stroking me too close to the edge.

"Do you like that, lover?"

Yeah, she actually asked me that. Would have served her right if I'd answered it was "good". I said stupid things sometimes but I'm not an idiot.

It was time to turn the tables anyway. I knew I wouldn't be satisfied until she came first. Maybe even second and third, if I could keep my own control for that long.

There was nothing weird or unnatural to having her sit on the edge of the bed so I could kneel between her spread thighs and lick her sweet pussy. She opened right up for me, giving me every drop I craved.

It wasn't enough. I needed her complete abandon.

I got it by sucking her clit into my mouth and when I had her full attention, using my tongue to stimulate her into next Tuesday. I was almost mean about it, refusing to let go or give her a rest until her pops started coming further and further apart. You know, like how you know the microwave popcorn is done.

Brave woman she was, she offered herself up to a good fucking at that point but I knew she wouldn't come again if I pounded her like I so desperately wanted to. It was the thought of feeling one of her ginormous orgasms clenching around my dick that kept me under control.

Then she begged for it and I almost lost it anyway. Fuckin' A, could there be anything sexier than the woman you love begging you to fuck her? Wait, there was. Making her go crazy as you gave it to her.

There was only one way to keep both of us from losing control too quickly. I maneuvered us so we were both on our sides, reached down to guide my way, then slowly pushed inside her as deeply as the position would allow.

Slow and easy...*oh yeah*... God, she was so hot and slick, swollen from her orgasms...slow and easy... *Oh, Fuck!*

I was a goner. She was moving with me, rubbing

against me with all that soft skin, her nipples poking my chest each time our bodies came together. One last coherent thought shot to my brain as my cum shot deep into Faith's welcoming pussy, *Next time.*

Next time we'd take it slow and easy. Next time I'd keep it together long enough to collect on that offered blowjob. Next time I'd lose control again and be perfectly happy to make the same promises. It really didn't matter. The only thing that mattered was that there would always *be* a next time.

I didn't bother pulling out as we snuggled and started to drift off to sleep.

Chapter Twenty
Marriage, Faith-style

The next morning while he was still asleep, I ran hot water in the bathtub and hit caller ID on Dorian's cell phone. Up came the last number called. It was in NJ, so I imagined it must be either the club, Guy or Juliet. With luck it *wouldn't* be Juliet! I hit the redial and waited.

A female voice asked, "Dorian?"

Frig. Now I hoped it *was* Juliet. It didn't sound like her and the last thing I wanted to do was speed dial one of his subs. After a couple of silent seconds, she repeated herself. "Hello? Dorian? Is that you?"

The voice sounded familiar. What the heck. I'd try a little fishing expedition and see what happened.

"Ah, no. This is Faith."

"Faith?" After a short pause, she recognized the name to my relief. "Oh…Faith! Of course. How are the outfits working out? Have you learned to walk in those heels?"

It was Suzanne. "Ah…well, not so much. I wasn't

really calling for another walking lesson. I was just um…hoping that Dorian remembered to thank you and let you and everyone know we'll be staying in Las Vegas."

"Permanently?"

"Maybe. We're getting married."

"Yes, I know. He told me. Congratulations! You have a wonderful man and I hope you appreciate him. A lot of men wouldn't do what he did."

"Uh…which thing that he did do you mean?"

"Calling all of his old subs to say goodbye. That was a classy thing to do. A lot of men wouldn't bother."

"Oh, of course. That. Yes, he's a gem and I'll treasure him—I promise."

"Good. Tell him we'll miss him."

"I will. *Yeah, right.* He's out getting fitted for a tux at the moment and I still haven't found the right dress. Could I ask you a big favor?"

"Of course."

"Could you let everyone know we're not coming back? It could save us some time. I'm pretty busy as you can imagine."

"Oh, yes. That would be easy."

"Thank you. We both appreciate it. We're hoping to get married this evening so we have plenty to do."

"It's no problem at all. I have Guy's private number and he can call Juliet. I'm sure they'll let the guests know as they ask for him."

"That would be terrific. Thanks, Suzanne! And don't hesitate to call if you need a favor."

"I won't. And please look me up if you come back to visit."

"Oh, we will. For sure." Note to self. No long

visits back home.

"Have a wonderful wedding, darling!"

"Thank you. 'Bye."

"Goodbye."

I hung up and deleted all the numbers.

* * * * *

Yes, we were really doing it. Getting married, I mean. We returned to our hotel after picking up the marriage license and as soon as Dorian booked the chapel, we did some much needed shopping. Toiletries, clothing, shoes with kitten heels…

He had a hard time understanding why we hadn't packed much of anything. The whole "two kids, so crazy in love, impulsively running off to Vegas to get married" story seemed to satisfy him. In fact, it seemed to please him tremendously.

Ivan had told us about a gigantic shopping mall only a cab ride away but neither one of us felt up to that challenge. A few clothing stores had been built right into our hotel as well as a few more out on the street. Basically, right where we were we could purchase anything from three-piece suits and evening gowns to stripper wear *for the honeymoon.*

We decided to discuss the rest of our plans while we walked around and checked out the stores.

"I know you had the whole, big, white wedding planned, Faith. I'm sorry if you always dreamed it would be like that. Are you disappointed?"

"Hell no," I said and laughed. "My mother planned that monstrosity of a wedding, right down to the groom and the last curl in my hair. I couldn't even get a Brazilian wax for fear that she'd try to glue the hairs back on. No, I'm thrilled to be able to do something more fun and free."

"Really?" His voice sounded strained, as if he didn't believe me.

"Yeah, really. Hey, the important thing is that I have the right guy."

"You sure do."

He leaned over and kissed me. It was only a peck but enough to make me go all warm inside. "I guess we'd better duck into a store and see what we can find." I tipped my head toward a place that looked promising.

"Sounds good." He held the door for me. Man, I loved this Dorian. I kinda hoped the other one had been permanently replaced—even though I loved him too. Was I in any way normal?

"Oh, wait! You can't see my dress before the wedding."

"You're kidding. You want Elvis to walk you down the aisle but I can't see your dress?"

"Hey, my father might forgive me if I can tell him a celebrity took his place."

Dorian laughed, pulled me close and kissed my forehead. "If you say so."

"So…are you okay with my going in here by myself and you looking for your suit somewhere else? I can meet you back at the room."

"I thought we were going to decide the details of our honeymoon while we shopped?"

"Oh, yeah! That reminds me, I need to get a whole trousseau. Don't expect me to get back right away."

He groaned and rolled his eyes.

"Just kidding. And I think we *know* what to do on our honeymoon." I winked.

He growled and nipped my neck, making me want to start the honeymoon early. I had to reluctantly push him away with a stern look. After he wandered off, I had the best time shopping. I knew he had excellent taste but *this* girl wanted *something* to be all about her. So picking the right dress suddenly took on major importance.

When I found *the one*, I nearly giggled out loud. A beautiful red satin cocktail dress with almost as many rhinestones outlining the deep, heart-shaped cleavage as Elvis would have on his belt. And it looked awesome on me. *Take that, Mother!* The saleslady even found me some red, open toed shoes with moderate heels and pretty rhinestone baubles.

Now I couldn't wait for the big evening. Ivan and Nina would be our witnesses, Elvis would walk me down the aisle and Dorian's jaw would drop when he saw me decked out in my gorgeous outfit. This is what they mean when they say, "It's your day."

I wished Kat could be here but she'd get a kick out of the video we were having made—and she'd be thrilled that I married for love.

Chapter Twenty and a Half
How Dorian spent his day

I had to remind myself to breathe. Everything was in motion and going fine until she said the words, "Brazilian wax". I actually had to wipe a bit of drool off my chin. No doubt the little minx would go and have it done just to drive me nuts knowing what was waiting for me under her clothes. The honeymoon would be soon enough to tell her how much seeing her pussy bare would turn me on, when I could make sure the only thing she covered up with was my mouth or my own short hairs.

Thankfully she got it in her head that I shouldn't see her dress before the wedding, so we split up and agreed to meet back at the room. I needed that time to get the image she'd placed out of my head.

I was back in the hotel room long before her. I knew she'd expect me to wear black, so I chose a gray suit. Hey, it was neutral but unexpected. I had a harder time with the tie but the second the sales guy asked me what color I thought of when I thought of my fiancée, I knew red was the right choice. When they were laid in front of me, I instantly knew which red too.

Then all the way back to the hotel, I was convinced Faith had chosen to wear green. Or purple. Or to make an extra stop for a Brazilian wax.

Oh, man. Had I groaned out loud? I wiped the drool off again and acknowledged that it was possible to get strange looks while walking down a street in Vegas.

Chapter Twenty-One

A picture-perfect wedding—well, almost

The chapel had been selected from pictures on a website. Despite the cheesy reputation of Vegas weddings, this place had some class. A long white runner scattered with silk rose petals led to the nondenominational altar covered with a beautiful bouquet. The flowers even looked real.

I hadn't seen it except in pictures since I had been shuffled into a changing room the minute I arrived. I guess I wasn't the only bride who didn't want the groom to see her all spiffed up before the actual wedding.

Now, I waited, *all shook up* in the lobby with "Elvis". You'd worry if I wasn't nervous, right? Well, *good,* because I literally trembled. I think that may have had more to do with the fact that I couldn't help thinking about my mother. Elvis didn't help by telling me how easy divorce was if things didn't work out— and, with a wink, that I knew where to find him. What a pep talk.

The doors swung open and Elvis began to sing *Love Me Tender* as he sashayed down the aisle and I walked slowly beside him, carrying my single red rose. Okay, it was a cute idea when we discussed it earlier but…

Dorian. There he stood in a gray suit and red tie that matched my gown as if they had been made from the same bolt of fabric. How the hell did he know what color I'd pick? Despite wanting him to be the one whose jaw dropped, I think mine hit the floor before his did. God, he was *gorgeous.*

I felt hot tears well up behind my eyes and prayed they wouldn't spill. It's one thing to get emotional at a beautiful, five-star, wedding-planner ceremony but this? Suddenly I was on the verge of laughing. I think this is what they call hysteria.

Dorian's cut figure blurred as my eyes filled. I wanted to run to him. I wanted to pinch myself just to be sure the whole thing was real. Damn, I wanted to get this over with and proceed straight to the honeymoon.

Ivan and Nina sat up front on the left. Fredrico and some woman I hadn't met sat on the right. Somehow I managed to stay with Elvis until he took my hand and placed it within my lover's grasp. Dorian's tight, warm grip relaxed me while we waited for Elvis's big finish.

When the last note echoed in my mind he moved off to the side, leaving the two of us standing before a Justice of the Peace. Everything seemed surreal. A cool, fresh smell met my nose and I became aware of the flowers. They were actually real—not plastic and dust covered as I'd expected. I guess when weddings are big business, they can afford a few nice extras.

Like the video camera behind the altar aimed at us, or the limo taking us back to our hotel. We had been moved to the honeymoon suite at Dorian's insistence. So what I'm saying is, it wasn't half bad as spur of the moment weddings go.

Someone's voice dragged my attention back to reality. Ah yes. The Justice of the Peace said a few words about love. It was from Corinthians, I think. Love is patient, love is kind, love will wait if you lose your mind… No. That last part was from my own scatterbrained imagination.

Dorian looked over at me and smiled. It helped. Squeezing my hand helped. Just being here with him instead of Roger helped. Wondering how I'd explain this all to my mother didn't help.

I dragged myself back to the moment, again, just as Dorian was asked those special questions. You know…the vows. He said, "I do" with no hesitation. How the heck did he do that? I hoped I could do that. I hoped the Justice didn't ask me if I'd obey—or wear makeup and always do the dishes right after dinner.

Whew. All he wanted me to promise was to love, honor and cherish. Yep, I could do that.

"I do."

Dorian placed a wide gold band on my ring finger and suddenly, as if by magic, Faith Daniels became Mrs. Dorian Markoff.

Smash!

The doors to the lobby burst open and the unexpected wedding crasher shrieked, "Stop! Hold everything!"

Thundering down the aisle, a raging bull named Juliet charged. Elvis jumped in front of me and said,

"Now hold on here, little lady…"

Little lady? She was as intimidating as The Terminator! A moment later the "little lady" punched him so hard his aviator sunglasses flew off.

"What the hell have you done to my Dorian?" she cried.

"Your Dorian?" There must have been an echo. Either that or about four people said the same thing at almost the same time.

I gaped at the person I thought was *my* Dorian and noted that he stared in wordless horror at Juliet.

"Okay, the Truss Club's Dorian. But I'm the one who's perfect for him," Juliet shouted.

Light dawned slowly. "Wait a minute… You wanted Dorian?"

"Damn right. Who wouldn't? I've come to get him back before he does something he'll regret."

Dorian found his voice at last. "I'm sorry, Miss, but I have no idea who you are or what you're talking about. And even if I did, Faith and I are already married, so you're too—"

"What?" She screeched.

"You're. Too. Late," I enunciated for her.

She lunged, screamed something unintelligible and then the words, "This time you die" quite clearly!

Dorian grabbed her shoulder, threw her off balance and she went down with a thud—and a fart. I scrambled out of her way, thanking God I had the sense to wear a dress she couldn't easily reach out and grab hold of and shoes I could run in. I took off and yelled over my shoulder as I ran, "Meet me at the car, darling."

Dorian nodded, then looked down at Juliet and she reached for him. Suddenly he bolted down the aisle and out the door right beside me. Man, he could move!

We jumped into the waiting limo and Dorian yelled, "Drive!"

The limo driver either sensed the urgency or this had happened before because he raced out of the parking lot with squealing tires.

We sped away with no destination in mind other than our future together. By the time we hit a straightaway, the pounding of my heart began to diminish.

Dorian raked his fingers through his hair. "Are you all right?"

"Yeah, I'm fine."

"What the hell was all that about?"

"Um…would you believe me if I said I have no idea?"

He leveled his eyes and just stared at me with his, *Do you think I'm an idiot?* look.

"Okay, okay…but I'm afraid this is going to be a lengthy explanation."

He groaned and flopped backward against the seat.

Chapter Twenty-One and a Half
Like Romeo and...Juliet? I'll take Faith

I was having an Elvis sighting and I couldn't take my eyes off the beautiful bride. God, she was perfect and yes, she'd chosen red. I never should have doubted that for a moment, knowing her inside and out so well. It was unbelievable that in such a short time I'd found someone I was willing to share my life with, that I could be completely up-front with and not have to worry that she wouldn't love me for who I am. I mean, I had plenty of money and all that but my life wasn't exactly out of the ordinary.

Well, if one didn't count the fact that I was marrying a woman I'd known only a week and she was being given away by Elvis, The Later Years.

Everyone had to have a little excitement in their lives, right? Besides, the second I laid eyes on her, I knew we were doing the right thing. We belonged together. With her hand in mine, I'd said the vows that would make it legal. I had to hold my breath until she'd said them too and then I'd pushed the simple band of gold past the knuckles of her ring finger and she was mine.

It was a beautiful moment but when it ended, all I could think was, "To the honeymoon!"

As if on cue, the doors to the lobby burst open, only it wasn't to let us out. It was to let one very angry woman in yelling, "Stop! Hold everything!"

Great. Of all the chapels to choose from, we'd ended up in one where someone decided to play out a scene from *The Graduate*. Too bad she'd gotten her time or place mixed up.

Shit. She took out Elvis. Then she yelled something that made no sense whatsoever, "What the hell have you done to my Dorian?"

"Your Dorian?" The question was a chorus, though I'd bet no one was more surprised than me to hear my name coming out of her mouth. I could only stare at her, wondering why she was trying to ruin my wedding and how the hell she could know me without my remembering her. She'd be kind of hard to miss. She was wearing a leather bra with tassels...over a completely sheer blouse. The short leather skirt and spiked alligator boots didn't help either.

I somehow found my voice right as she reached us. "I'm sorry, Miss but I have no idea who you are or what you're talking about. And even if I did, Faith and I are already married, so you're too—"

"*What?*" she screeched.

"You're. Too. Late," Faith said more slowly, with just enough taunt to make me realize that she knew the woman.

Double shit. The woman heard the taunt too and lunged for Faith, threatening to kill her. Interestingly enough, it didn't appear to be the first time she'd tried.

I took the woman down. It was harder than I thought, given the stiletto boots and the fact that she wanted to kill Faith but I could have done without the giant fart that accompanied the solid thud. It was definitely time to go.

Faith was on the same wavelength and was already headed for the limo. Good, because we needed to be alone.

My wife had some explaining to do.

Chapter Twenty-Two
Faith comes clean

It took quite a while to answer all of his questions and even longer before he believed me but every now and then I'd see a light of recognition in his eyes. I'm sure it was a lot to take in. At last he stopped pacing and stood in front of the window of our bridal suite, looking out at the brightly lit Las Vegas night.

"So, I had this whole secret BDSM life back in New Jersey that I don't remember."

"Yes."

"And you were going to arrest me for the business I own. I'm the owner of a place called The Truss Club?"

"Yes."

He turned and frowned at me. "Why didn't you? Why did you marry me instead?"

"Because I love you."

He shook his head at the ceiling. "But according to what you told me, I kidnapped you, drugged you, brought you here against your will in order to wipe your mind—"

"And yours got wiped instead."

"Right. I'm not doubting that part. It explains the gaps in my memory. But what I don't get is why you'd love the bastard who did this to you."

"Well…you also saved my life."

"I did?"

"Yeah, Juliet wanted to give me a pair of cement shoes and toss me in the river to sleep with the fishes."

He strolled over and sat next to me on the bed. "Well, I'm glad I didn't let her do that."

"So am I."

He snaked his arm around my waist and kissed me. It wasn't one of his toe-curling kisses but I tingled just the same.

When he pulled away, he seemed puzzled again. "So you went along with the hypnosis idea, knowing it might have worked on you and not me."

"Yes."

He took my hand and kissed it. "You must love me a lot."

"I do."

"And I love you. I may not be sure of much right now but I am sure of that."

Every time he said he loved me I went all warm and gooey inside. Yup. I loved him like crazy but I still shook in my shoes at the thought of telling my mother about us.

"What is it? You look worried."

"Huh? Oh, yeah. I was just worrying about what my mother is going to say when I tell her I married a Gentile."

He sat up a little straighter. "What makes you

think I'm a Gentile?"

"Well…I uh…" *Holy smokes!* I'd never asked him his religion. I just assumed… "Aren't you?"

"No. Technically, my mother was Jewish."

My jaw dropped. *No way. I must be hallucinating. My mind is just making this up.* After a full thirty seconds of probing his eyes and finding no hint of guile behind them, I cracked up and went right into hysterics.

He smiled. "What's so funny?"

"Are you sure you're Jewish? You're too good in bed."

"I don't think that has anything to do with religion."

"I can only judge by experience and I've had painfully little of it. I thought you were the only non-Jew I'd ever slept with."

"Nope. Like I said, my mother was Jewish and she insisted we know that part of our heritage."

"Not Orthodox, I assume."

He looked at me like I was nuts. "Do you see a beard and dreadlocks? I'm as unorthodox as they come."

"In more ways than one. Why didn't you ever tell me?"

"You didn't ever ask."

Chapter Twenty-Two and a Half
Dorian forgives and the groom accepts his wife

I looked out at the brightly lit Las Vegas night, noting that the Stratosphere stood out like a beacon. Yep, still phallic. I suppose we should have had our wedding there, considering what Faith was telling me.

"So, I had this whole secret BDSM life back in New Jersey that I don't remember." I summed it up as best I could.

"Yes."

"And you were going to arrest me for the business I own. I'm the owner of a place called The Truss Club?"

"Yes."

Okay, now I was getting the honesty I thought I'd had all along. It hurt that she'd kept this secret from me but she'd also married me after I'd kidnapped her, drugged her and tried to erase her memory. How could I sit in judgment of *her*?

I asked a few more questions but they all led to the only answer that made any sense. The only answer that mattered. I took her hand and kissed it. "You must love me a lot."

"I do."

"And I love you. I may not be sure of much right now but I am sure of that."

She got that look on her face that made me want to drop everything, including our clothes. Then Faith Markoff did what she did best. She surprised me. All this time, on top of everything else, she had been willing to face her mother and tell her, "Tough shit, my husband isn't Jewish and you'll just have to deal with it."

Only she didn't have to do that because I am. Don't get me wrong, I still wasn't crazy about having to face her mother but I was definitely getting the feeling no sane man would be looking forward to that. Not without an MD or PhD after their name and I knew having the initials stand for Master Dom or Pleasurable Hurt Doctor wouldn't count.

If it meant I could spend my days and nights with Faith, I'd slay—er, meet the dragon with a smile. But that was for another day.

We had a marriage to consummate.

"I have two questions for you, wife." I stood and began to remove my clothing, watching her eyes widen when I reached for my belt. "Okay, three questions. But I'm not going to start asking them until you're naked too."

"Is that a threat?" She looked at my bare chest like she could enjoy the show all night.

"You want it to be?" I countered. "I'm already ahead of you and if I'm naked before you are, I'll make sure I *finish* before you. If that's not clear enough, instead of the hours and hours of orgasmic delight only one of us is capable of, I'll…"

She whipped the dress over her head, kicked off her shoes and was naked. All of her. She'd found the time for a Brazilian wax.

My mouth watered as I shed the rest of my clothes and toppled her onto the bed, loving the feel of all that soft, smooth skin stretched out beneath me.

"First question," I made myself ask as I nipped her neck, then nuzzled the spot. "Will my memory ever come back?"

"Maybe." She lifted her knees and cradled my hips. "But we don't have to wait to see. Fredrico can probably undo the hypnosis anytime."

In a move that nearly had my eyes crossing, she lifted her hips, rubbing our groins together. "It's up to you."

Oh, it was up all right. And two could play at that game. Reaching down, I positioned my dick right over her clit and gave her one long, gliding stroke through the already wet lips of her pussy. "Question two…"

"Dorian! Shut up and fuck me!"

I let my smile tell her that was not going to happen, then I captured her hands in mine and pressed them to the bed. She growled in frustration but her quivering body said she liked it. I liked it too and it felt oddly comfortable, which reminded me of the need for the second question. "Did I do any Dom stuff with you? I mean, other than kidnapping you and drugging you and all."

"What, like spank me or whip me? You still have your cock, don't you?"

I laughed even as I shuddered at the thought. Right, stupid question but I was a bit nervous when she eyed my belt like that after telling me I was into that stuff.

"We agreed to respect each other. No hitting."

I nodded, remembering that. "Question three…"

"You have got to be kidding—mmf!"

I took her mouth in what turned into a kiss so carnal we were both writhing and groaning by the time I pulled back. I didn't go far, just enough to be able to see her face.

"Open your eyes, Faith," I demanded. She did and the love and lust I saw in their depths nearly did me in. "Have we ever made love, just us, no games, no mental or physical barriers?"

"C-close. Condom between us." She found her breath. "But we didn't erase any of our sex life. Everything you remember really happened."

Okay, so that was a major relief to know. And now I knew we'd be creating many new memories with what I had planned. Maybe even something more.

I shifted and widened her spread legs, our fingers still entwined by her head. I was in no hurry as our bodies rubbed and stroked in all the right places until I felt the slick heat of her opening against the sensitive tip of my dick.

"Then feel me on our wedding night, wife. All of me."

I pressed hard, seating to the hilt in one thrust.

Faith sucked in a deep breath but I was the one who cried out her name. God, she was so hot, so tight and wet I nearly went out of my mind. I closed my eyes and kissed her again, hoping it would help somehow.

That's when she came.

I hadn't moved, couldn't move for fear of coming too but it didn't matter to her. She had one of her ginormous orgasms that you're damn straight I remembered, only I'd never felt it like this. Her inner muscles tightened like a vise, caressing my cock, flooding around me with even more heat before tightening again. And again.

I held on, determined to make love to my wife for hours on end. Shit, why hadn't I jumped on the tantric sex craze like I'd thought about doing? I hadn't, so I could only groan as she clenched me again, drenched me again, called my name in ecstasy. God help me, I held on.

"Dorian."

She'd exhaled it that time. I opened my eyes to find her watching me, supreme satisfaction in her gaze but we were completely connected and I could feel her yearning too. Her fingers tightened in mine and she lifted her hips in invitation.

Then she smiled and I knew I was done for. "I love you. Come for me, Dorian."

That did it. My name was still halfway from her lips when I felt a fireball gather at my spine and shoot through my dick into her waiting pussy. There was no time to thrust but I did helplessly grind against her and I must have caught her clit because holy shit, she screamed and started clenching me again. That, her heat, my heat and knowing what I was doing to her were all it took for another fireball to start rolling.

All in all, it was a hell of a wedding night.

Epilogue

And they all lived kinkily ever after

You didn't think I was going to let my husband have the last word, did you? Ha! Of course not. You know me too well.

We returned to New Jersey, set up housekeeping

in Dorian's gorgeous glass house and I tried not to throw stones, or coffeepots. I'm not a morning person. But after a year, any differences we had were ironed out. Speaking of ironing, I've even got a frickin' housekeeper! That and a few other nice perks will keep me happy for the next forty or fifty years.

What are those other perks? Well, Dorian had to become a silent partner in the Truss Club. He's still collecting his third but Juliet and Guy manage the whole thing. I swore to maintain a code of silence about it. Even if I blew the whistle, so to speak, I can't testify against my husband. Therefore it was decided for the club's protection—and mine from Juliet—that Dorian remain a secret owner. They even moved its location, upon my recommendation to somewhere *not* across the street from a police station and a block away from a synagogue.

He really is an independent investor now. He discovered a brilliant inventor who needed about thirty thousand dollars to start up his company. For Dorian, that was petty cash. The man he invested in has made some wonderful advances in assisted living facilities, so think of us when your parents retire to West Palm Beach—like mine did. *Big* yay!

Speaking of my parents…

Dorian, being his ever charming self, won them over in a heartbeat.

My dad? The furniture king? He was so damn impressed with Dorian's house, car and status as a successful investor, he almost abdicated his crown. Almost. He may have sold the business to his nephew, my cousin Ari, but he's still the patriarch. Or at least we let him think so. He issues edicts from his throne by the swimming pool and we do as we please.

Thus our time-honored traditions are maintained.

Oh and he wasn't amused by my replacing him with Elvis, so we had to do the whole wedding over again. But this time it was a small, family-only affair in a function room of a restaurant with a progressive rabbi officiating. Very nice, very low-key, very Jewish. Now, according to my mother, we're really married.

And what ever happened to Roger? Well, as it turns out, my running out on that wedding was the best thing for both of us. He and my cousin Ari were married in Massachusetts and he's now the furniture queen.

So what am I doing now, you ask? Am I still a cop? What are you, nuts? Having the attention span of a gnat and being prone to rash actions, I was clearly never cut out for the job. No, my new job actually helps me focus and builds patience. I design and make my own jewelry. Suzanne sells it in her upscale boutique. Sometimes I throw in something a little kinky like sterling silver nipple clamps and test them myself to make sure they work. Oh yeah. We're still trying it every which way.

So when I'm not working, shopping, getting my nails done or bossing around the housekeeper, we're busy getting laid. That last part is still my favorite "chore"—snort. There's plenty of passion and spice, which we intend to keep.

There's one little problem I can't fix, thanks to Wolfie but it may just come in handy someday. I can hardly wait to freak out our kids by knowing everything they whisper behind closed doors.

About the Authors

Ashlyn Chase: Kidnapped by gypsies as an infant, Ashlyn was left on the doorstep of the Massachusetts home in which she grew up—at least that's what her older siblings told her. It seems that storytelling runs in the family.

Ashlyn worked as a psychiatric nurse for several years, holds a degree in behavioral sciences and has been trained as a fine artist, registered nurse, hypnotherapist, and interior designer.

Most writers, whether they're aware of it or not, have a "theme", some sort of thread that runs through all of their books, uniting the whole mishmash into an identifiable signature. Ashlyn's identified her theme as involving characters who reinvent themselves. It's no wonder, since she has reinvented herself numerous times. Finally content with her life, she lives in beautiful Florida with her true-life superhero husband, Mr. Amazing.

Dalton Diaz: If a story doesn't have romance, it isn't worth it. If there's hot sex, it's extra worth it. The only thing that can make it better from there is humor.

Let's face it, fantasy is usually a lot more fun than reality. Not always, but usually. As a writer, one can be anything, do anything, say anything that comes to mind. There are a thousand and one ways to make things happen, each one more exciting than the last.

Tell Me What You Think

I appreciate hearing reader opinions. You can email me at ash@ashlynchase.com
Or better yet, leave a review at the online retailer where you bought the book!
Speaking of buying books, here's a universal link to all my books and online booksellers:
https://www.books2read.com/ap/ngobln/Ashlyn-Chase

Ashlyn communicates with fans regularly via social media. Her newsletter list just keeps growing. Sign up at her website http://ashlynchase.com
or directly here: https://tinyurl.com/y6lzesr7

More places to check out:
https://bookbub.com/authors/ashlyn-chase
Twitter https://twitter.com/#!/GoddessAsh
Facebook http://facebook.com/authorashlynchase
Instagram https://.instagram.com/ashlynlaughin/
Pinterest https://pinterest.com/ashlynchase/
Blogger http://ashlynchase.blogspot.com/
Have fun with Ash and friends at:
http://groups.yahoo.com/group/ashlynsnewbestfriends/

Don't forget to register for the Fall in Love with New England reader/author conference!
http://fallinlovewithnewengland.com

Also by Ashlyn Chase

--Phoenix Brothers series--
A Phoenix is Forever, Sourcebooks 3/2019
More than a Phoenix, Sourcebooks 9/2018
Hooked on a Phoenix, Sourcebooks 3/2018
--Boston Dragons series--
Never Dare a Dragon, Sourcebooks 9/2017
My Wild Irish Dragon, Sourcebooks 4/2017
I Dream of Dragons, Sourcebooks 4/2016
--Be Careful What You Summon duo—
Tiger's Night Out, Imagination Unlimited 1/2019
Vampire Vintage, Imagination Unlimited 1/2015
--Stand Alones--
Wonder B*tch, Imagination Unlimited 6/2018
Laura's Upcycled Life, Imagination Unlimited 2017
Immortally Yours, Imagination Unlimited 4/2017
Thrill of the Chase, Imagination Unlimited 4/2017
Gods Gone Wild, Imagination Unlimited, 11/2015
--Love Spells Gone Wrong series--
Out of the Broom Closet, Lachesis Publishing 2/2016
Tug of Attraction, Lachesis Publishing 9/2015
The Cupcake Coven, Lachesis Publishing 6/2015
--Flirting with Fangs series--
Kissing with Fangs, Sourcebooks 3/2014
How to Date a Dragon, Sourcebooks 9/2013
Flirting Under a Full Moon, Sourcebooks 4/2013
--Strange Neighbors series--
The Vampire Next Door, Sourcebooks 8/2011
The Werewolf Upstairs, Sourcebooks: 2/2011
Strange Neighbors, Sourcebooks: 6/2010
--Heaving Bosoms/Quivering Thighs duo--
Quivering Thighs, Imagination Unlimited 6/2015
Heaving Bosoms, Imagination Unlimited 6/2015

53719114R00140

Made in the
USA
Lexington, KY